Literary Walks of Britain

'Had I not sat on Painswick Hill
With a nymph upon my knees ...'

Literary Walks of Britain

Edited and with an Introduction by Donald Veall
With photographs by Simon McBride

Webb & Bower
MICHAEL JOSEPH

First published in Great Britain 1989 by
Webb & Bower (Publishers) Limited
9 Colleton Crescent, Exeter, Devon EX2 4BY
in association with Michael Joseph Limited
27 Wright's Lane, London W8 5TZ

Penguin Books Ltd, Registered Offices: Harmondsworth, Middlesex,
England
Viking Penguin Inc, 40 West 23rd Street, New York, New York 10010,
USA
Penguin Books Australia Ltd, Ringwood, Victoria, Australia
Penguin Books Canada Ltd, 2801 John Street, Markham, Ontario,
Canada L3R 1DA
Penguin Books (NZ) Ltd, 182-190 Wairau Road, Auckland 10, New
Zealand

Designed by Peter Wrigley

Production by Nick Facer/Rob Kendrew

Introduction and selection Copyright © 1989 Donald Veall
Photographs Copyright © 1989 Simon McBride/Webb & Bower
(Publishers) Limited

British Library Cataloguing in Publication Data

Literary walks of Britain.
    1. English literature. Special subjects.
    Places. Anthologies
    I. Veall, Donald
    820.8′032

    ISBN 0–86350–286–5

Typeset in Great Britain by Keyspools Limited, Golborne, Lancashire
Colour reproduction produced by Mandarin Offset in Hong Kong
Printed and bound in Hong Kong

TO JANE

I wish to thank my wife Jane and Valerie Mendes for their
critical help. I would also like to express my appreciation to
Margaret McCully and Edie Souter for their secretarial
assistance with the manuscript.

Unfortunately this work must now be published posthumously, as Donald died in August 1987. I would like to
thank the publishers for their help in finalizing the
presentation. Perhaps I should add that the original
inspiration for this anthology was Emily Brontë's poem:
Come walk with me.

Jane Barnett Veall.

CONTENTS

Come, walk with me,
    There's only thee
To bless my spirit now –
    We used to love on winter nights

To wander through the snow;
    Can we not woo back old delights?
The clouds rush dark and wild,
    They fleck with shade our mountain heights
The same as long ago
    And on the horizon rest at last
In looming masses piled;
    While moonbeams flash and fly so fast
We scarce can say they smiled.

Come walk with me – come, walk with me;
    We were not once so few,
But death has stolen our company
    As sunshine steals the dew.
He took them one by one and we
    Are left the only two;
So closer would my feelings twine
    Because they have no stay but thine.

EMILY BRONTË

INTRODUCTION

Walking evokes a different response in different people. This anthology is intended to illustrate how writers and poets have felt about walking in all its varied forms. 'There is no orthodoxy in walking' wrote GM Trevelyan: 'It is a land of many paths and no paths, where everyone goes his own way and is right.'

No ancient Greek or Roman has been recorded as going on a walking tour. A sixteenth-century French poet, Pierre de Ronsard, told in a poem how he loved gardens that retained some wildness. There he could talk with a friend, read or fall asleep amidst the flowers. If the weather was threatening or overcast he could seek out company, play poker, ride, jump, wrestle, fence, tell jokes, make love or talk with women. An athletic and energetic man, yet the last thing that would have occurred to him would be to go for a walk. Walking was not regarded as something undertaken for pleasure but only as a means of going somewhere in particular when there was no alternative.

Many years ago, it was often the case that to walk meant a man could not afford to ride. The grand tours of the eighteenth century, which might extend one, two or three years, were undertaken by the wealthy and the leisured who rode in their carriages. Walking was regarded as the poor man's way of getting about, to be avoided whenever possible. The nearest to walking for the well-to-do was going for a stroll along laid out walks in private country seats – not across other people's land. Thomas Hobbes (1588–1697), the philosopher, did much of his thinking whilst he strolled in his patron's park and he had an ink-horn fitted into his staff so that he could jot down ideas when they occurred to him. Marie-Antoinette, confined for the greater part of her adult life to royal residences, often strolled in the private parks attached to the royal palaces at Versailles and Fontainebleau,

particularly in the grounds of Le Petit Trianon, a small château given to her by her husband.

Probably the most famous literary walker was William Wordsworth (1770–1850). He must have spent more time walking than any other man of letters. Much of his work was inspired by his walking. De Quincey calculated that Wordsworth, by the time he was sixty-five, some fifteen years before his death, had walked nearly 180,000 miles, 'a mode of exertion which, to him, stood in the stead of alcohol and all the stimulants.' There is a story that when living at Racedown (between Crewkerne and Lyme in Dorset), Wordsworth rode a horse to Lyme. Whilst he was there he forgot he had a horse and walked back to Racedown.

Wordsworth's lifelong habit was to compose his poetry whilst walking out of doors whether in his own orchard, beside the lakes or along the fells. Whilst composing Wordsworth often spoke the lines aloud

like a river murmuring
And talking to itself

Dorothy Wordsworth in her *Journals* describes how William 'walks out every morning, generally alone, and brings in a large treat almost every time he goes out.' If it was wet he took an umbrella and walked up and down on a selected beat for hours. Whilst he was so engaged he seldom knew whether it was rain or fine. Poetic composition for Wordsworth was very much an oral affair; he chanted or (as his country neighbours described it) 'boomed' his verses aloud until the woods rang with his words.

Wordsworth went on numerous walking tours. In 1790, when aged twenty, he went on a tour across Europe with a Welshman, Robert Jones, each man's belongings tied up in a pocket handkerchief. They were probably the pioneers of those many ramblers and hikers who from that time to the present day have claimed the right to walk for pleasure over the countryside.

Wordsworth went round the Lake District with Coleridge; with Dorothy and Coleridge, he went on a tour of Scotland although they separated from Coleridge after a while. William, his wife Mary and sister Dorothy all went on a walking tour in the Alps. When he was sixty years old William did a walking tour of Scotland with his daughter, Dora, she often riding in a carriage while William walked beside her, usually covering twenty miles a day. When he was sixty-six, Wordsworth complained he was no longer able to walk all day; he could only manage six or seven hours.

Yet Wordsworth was also a poet of the town. When he lived in London in his youth in 1791, as recorded in *The Prelude*, he often walked around the streets at night in the winter 'when unwholesome rains are falling hard.' At other times he walked round, like Charles Dickens was to do later, to discover the myriad activities of a capital city – the performing animals, street singers, street artists, markets, prostitutes, begging scavengers, clowns, conjurors, ventriloquists, stone-eaters, fire swallowers, blind beggars, poverty stricken children and men and women from numerous foreign countries. Yet Wordsworth was conscious of the distance between himself and every one he saw and between the inhabitants themselves:

> the face of everyone
> that passes by me is a mystery.

Dorothy (1771–1855) was always ready to walk with William, as De Quincey noted, 'wet or dry, storm or sunshine, night or day.' A contemporary of theirs, Harriet Martineau, said 'Forty miles a day was not a singular feat of Dorothy's.'

William wrote of his sister:

> Nymph-like she is fleet and strong
> And down the rocks can leap along
> like rivulets in May
>
> She loves her fire, her cottage home;

> Yet o'er the moorland will she roam
> In weather rough and bleak.

In 1794 William and Dorothy went on a tour of the Wye Valley, covering fifty miles in three days, William composing *Lines composed a few miles above Tintern Abbey*, which he finished as they walked into Bristol in the evening. In 1799 William wrote to Coleridge how he and Dorothy had covered ten miles over a high mountain road with the wind behind them in two and a quarter hours and then, after a rest, covered seven miles in an hour and thirty-five minutes. When the Wordsworths moved house from Sockburn-on-Tees in County Durham to Grasmere they both walked the last three days of the journey in severe winter weather. They were both exhilarated and exhausted by the difficulties of the walk.

The Wordsworths regularly used to walk from Grasmere to Ambleside to collect the post, seven miles each way. If William was not at home Dorothy thought nothing of making the journey on foot alone. This was considered very unconventional and risky at that time. There was great prejudice against women rambling over the countryside. Tradition was against all respectable women taking short walks in the country and no 'lady' would have thought of indulging in a walking tour. Dorothy's great aunt severely reprimanded her for 'rambling about the country on foot.' In reply Dorothy wrote:

> So far from considering this as a matter of condemnation, I rather thought it would have given my friends pleasure to hear that I had the courage to make use of the strength which nature has endowed me, when it not only procured me infinitely more pleasure than I should have received from sitting in a post-chaise, but was also the means of saving me at least thirty shillings.

It was presumed that women were incapable of rigorous or sustained movement and of long exposure to the open air with the wind and the rain. In 1797 William Hutton in *Remarks upon North Wales* expressed his intense disapproval of seeing a woman who had walked up to the top of Snowdon with two men. The mountain was encircled in clouds but the woman was so elated with her achievement, even though she could see nothing, pulled off her hat and cap and 'huzzaed for joy.' Both cap and hat were carried away by the wind, much to Hutton's satisfaction.

Another lone woman walker, a contemporary of Dorothy Wordsworth, was Ellen Weeton (1776–?). She kept a journal and in 1809 wrote how she longed to go on a walking tour in Wales but dared not. She was afraid of 'the many insults a female is liable to, if alone.' Also her ignorance of the Welsh language was another obstacle. 'If I was but a man, now! I could soon do it.' She then went on to tell:

> A Miss Prescott of Leigh [in Wales], a singular character, once travelled to the south of England that way, taking London in her route, accompanied by a gentleman; which, as he was no way related, was worse than going alone, in the world's estimation. I am not *quite* so severe in my opinions, though I should not choose to do it myself.

Ellen Weeton had a sad life, marred by many misfortunes, but she did derive intense pleasure from walking. Her father died when she was very young and her mother had a struggle to make ends meet. She married at thirty-seven a widower who turned out to be an undisclosed bankrupt who bullied and ill-treated her and made off with what little money she possessed. A strong feminist, she asserted that men and women were equal and ought to be treated the same in every respect. 'Whoever censures woman as inferior to man debases himself.' Most of Ellen's walking was done alone. 'I choose to go alone, in places unfrequented by those of my own species, that my thoughts, as well as my feet, may ramble without restraint.' The one extract from her writings in this anthology is in fact an account of a group expedition up a mountain, Fairfield, 2,862 feet high near Grasmere.

In Ellen Weeton's *Journal of a Governess* she records how in the Isle of Man in the summer of 1812, when she was thirty-five, she walked 203 miles in just over three weeks, much of it hill and mountain walking. On one day she walked thirty-five miles in twelve hours. It was her normal practice on these walks to take a memo book with her to note down her observations and those ideas worth transcribing. Some thirteen years later she walked up Snowdon alone with the aid of a guide book, covering some twenty-five miles. She was fortunate on that occasion in that there was not a cloud to be seen although there was slight haze. It was on that visit to North Wales that she recorded how she could 'skip like a lamb amongst the rocks, and enjoy the sport, after a ten or twelve miles walk.' The previous year Ellen had spent eleven weeks in London sightseeing. She walked everywhere and records that she covered $538\frac{3}{4}$ miles during that time.

As a schoolboy Coleridge (1772–1834) described himself as 'having acquired an indisposition to all bodily activity . . . as I could not play at anything and was slothful, I was despised and hated by the boys.' Whatever truth there may be in those observations of his school days, as a man he was a good swimmer and an extraordinarily active walker. He went on numerous walking tours either alone or with a companion. He walked all round the lakes and mountains of the Lake District alone. It was usual at that time to traverse the more perilous parts with a guide – in so far as anybody then climbed mountains for sheer pleasure. In 1802 Coleridge ascended Scawfell Pike, the highest Lakeland mountain, whilst he was up there took notes and wrote a letter to the Wordsworths; then he rushed all the way down, avoiding the easier paths.

In 1804, when he was thirty-one, Coleridge walked from Grasmere to Kendal in bad weather covering some nineteen miles in four and a half hours. When Coleridge lived at Keswick he frequently visited the Wordsworths at Grasmere and thought nothing of the thirteen-mile mountainous walk over Dunmail Rise – sometimes he extended the walk by going over Helvellyn as well.

William Hazlitt, when he was twenty, went to visit Coleridge at Nether Stowey in Somerset. Hazlitt tells how he and John Chester went for a walk with Coleridge, and how Chester had to keep up a virtual trot beside Coleridge 'like a running footman beside a stage coach.'

In Coleridge's Scottish tour of 1803, after he left the Wordsworths, he walked 263 miles in eight days. This was achieved despite being in bad health; his stomach was 'brewing vinegar' and there was a suspicion of gout. Coleridge did meet his measure when he was fifty-six. He visited Charles Lamb at Enfield and stayed a week. Lamb, a small man with spindly legs, three years younger, insisted on walking Coleridge so incessantly through the lanes and byways of the vicinity that Coleridge acquired a pair of miserably sore feet and had to go to bed in consequence.

Walking provided Coleridge with an inspiration for writing. He liked to compose whilst walking over uneven ground or breaking through the straggling branches of a copse wood. He began composing *The Rhyme of the Ancient Mariner* when he was on a walk with William and Dorothy Wordsworth from Watchet to Lynton in 1797.

It was on that walk that Wordsworth also composed some of his early poems. The discussions which took place between Wordsworth and Coleridge (many of them whilst they were walking together) were momentous for English poetry. A new poetry emerged representing a revulsion from the neo-classicism of the eighteenth century to a renovation of the language of poetry.

In 1798 William Hazlitt (1778–1830) set out on a walking tour from Wem in Shropshire through Shrewsbury, Worcester, Upton, Tewkesbury, Gloucester, Bristol and Bridgwater to Nether Stowey to see Coleridge – a distance of some 150 to 160 miles. He also walked across England from Wem to Wisbech in Cambridgeshire. His passion for walking was an expression of his desire for physical exercise; he used to play racquets. When over forty he claimed he could walk forty to fifty miles a day for five or six hours at a time. For Hazlitt, as he wrote in his famous essay, *On Going a Journey:*

> ... the soul of a journey is liberty, perfect liberty to think, feel, do just as one pleases. We go on a journey chiefly to be free of all impediments and of all inconveniences; to leave ourselves behind, much more to get rid of others. It is because I want a little breathing space to muse on indifferent matters ... that I absent myself from the town for a while.

Charles Lamb's (1775–1834) approach to walking was in complete contrast to the nature lovers. Inveterate walker that he was, nature to him was dead, he was very much London living. He said he never tired of London 'all the bustle and wickedness about Covent Garden, the very women of the town, the watchmen, drunken scenes.' He said he ventured into the countryside for a while and as a break. 'I was born bred and passed most of my time in a crowd.' He wrote in 1802: 'This has begot in me an entire affection for that way of life, amounting to an almost insurmountable aversion from solitude and rural scenes.' His friend, Henry Crabb Robinson, told of how he and Lamb went for a walk from the Temple to Enfield via Southgate in 1814 after an early breakfast in Lamb's chambers:

> After tea ... we returned. The whole day most delightfully fine and the scenery very agreeable. Lamb enjoyed the walk more than the scenery, for the enjoyment of which he seems to have no great susceptibility. His great delight, even in preference to a country walk, is a stroll in London. The shops and the busy streets, such as Thames Street, Bankside, etc are his great favourites.

In later years there was some modification in Lamb's attitude. He moved out of London to what was then the village of Islington and later to Enfield and Edmonton, and he had a cottage at Button Snap in Hertfordshire. In a letter to his friend Robert Lloyd, when listing some of his likes, Lamb included 'a country walk.'

Wordsworth in a poem written after Lamb's death in his memory was to say:

> Thou went a scorner of the fields, my Friend
> But more in show than truth.

In his earlier years Charles Lamb walked much with his sister, Mary. They frequently walked thirty miles a day. After

Tintern Abbey, pre-Reformation home to Cistercian monks, has been immortalized in the poetry of William Wordsworth.

Lamb's retirement from the India House he wrote to Robert Southey 'Mary walks her twelve miles a day and I my twenty on other days.' In Lamb's later years Mary's health deteriorated and she could not accompany him. Lamb's adopted daughter, Emma Isola, became his walking companion. She probably found it hard work to keep up with Charles's demanding pace. Once he went on a twenty-four-mile walk with Emma. She arrived with feet so sore and blistered that her friends put her to bed for two days.

Some twenty years after expressing his love for London, Lamb wrote to Wordsworth in 1822:

> I have thought, in a green old age, to have retired to Ponder's End (emblematic name, how beautiful!) in the Ware Road, there to have made up my accounts with Heaven and the Company, toddling about between it and Cheshunt; anon stretching on some fine Isaac Walton morning to Hoddesdon or Amwell, careless as a beggar, but walking, walking ever, till I fairly walked myself off my legs, dying walking.

Lamb's passion for London remained with him all his life. In his last year he wrote to Thomas Manning: 'I walk nine or ten miles a day always up the road, dear Londonwards. Fields, flowers, birds and green lanes I have no heart for. The Ware Road is cheerful and almost as good as a street.'

In spite of being lame from infancy (he suffered from infantile paralysis), Walter Scott (1771–1832) as a boy of thirteen or fourteen delighted in long walks of twenty miles a day visiting all the old castles within reach of Edinburgh. At eighteen he was walking thirty miles a day at three miles an hour on day-long walks from five in the morning until eight in the evening. He would unhesitantly climb crags trusting to the strength of his arms to remedy his weakness. He would often disappear for days on end wandering the countryside much to his parents' anxiety. He particularly liked scenes that had historical associations. Mostly his walking was done with companions but sometimes he went off alone because of a love of solitude 'to indulge visions and airy castles of my own.' In

1805 on a visit to the Lake District, with Wordsworth and Humphrey Davey, the chemist, he went up the steep ascent of Helvellyn where there is a fine panorama over the surrounding countryside. Both Wordsworth and Scott wrote a poem on the subject of a young man who had lost his way on Helvellyn and died in a fall and was not found until three months later. Scott was as energetic physically in his walking, riding and coursing as he was mentally in his prolific writings in both verse and prose. Scotland for him was the

> Land of brown heath and shaggywood
> Land of the mountain and the flood,
> Land of my sires, what mortal hand
> Can e'er untie the filial band,
> That limits me to they rugged strand!

The walks enabled Scott to saturate his mind with the local traditions and scenery which he incorporated into his writing.

John Clare (1793–1864), a man without formal education, with illiterate parents, nevertheless became one of the finest of English country or native poets although it was not until the twentieth century that he came to be appreciated. Edward Thomas wrote of him: 'The poet consumed the labourer in him, or left only the dregs of one, while the conditions of the labourer's life were as a millstone about his neck.' He greatly resented the enclosure of the fields, greens, commons and the woods which restricted the right to wander in the countryside.

When once asked how he wrote his poetry Clare replied that it came to him whilst walking in the fields – that he kicked it out of the clods.

> Morning noon and gloaming
> I write my poems in these paths unseen

Clare wandered the fields of his native Northamptonshire alone with pencil and paper in his pocket, noting down his feelings in verse inspired by the moment. He would settle down in some quiet nook or corner and rapidly shape his imagination into words. One of his favourite places was the hollow of an oak on the orders of Helpston Heath, known as Lea Close Oak, where he had formed himself a seat with something like a table in front. When he returned home he would correct and polish his work if he decided he did not like it, he would destroy it.

Another nature poet, although of a very different kind, with a much more varied subject matter and from a very different background, who found walking a help in composing was Shelley (1792–1822). On his walks Shelley would take a notebook and have a favourite spot where he would sit down in the open air and compose. Sometimes he walked alone, at other times with his wife, Mary, her half-sister Claire or his various friends, Thomas Hogg, Thomas Love Peacock, Edward Williams or Edward Trelawney.

Mary wrote that Shelley

> … knew every plant by its name and was familiar with the history and habits of every production of the earth; he could interpret without a fault each appearance in the sky; and the varied phenomena of heaven and earth filled him with deep emotion. He made his study and reading room of the shadowed copse, the stream, the lake and the waterfall.

Shelley lived in many different places in England – he was always restless. His longest and perhaps happiest stay was in Marlow in 1817. He chose Marlow because he considered it no great distance from London and because it was on the Thames where he could indulge his passion for boating. It was here that Shelley composed his longest epic poem *The Revolt of Islam*. It was written whilst floating in his boat on the Thames or during his wanderings in the neighbourhood of Bisham Wood. Mary wrote that the neighbouring country was distinguished for peculiar beauty. 'The chalk hills break into cliffs that overhang the Thames, or from valleys clothed with beech; the wilder portion of the country is rendered beautiful by exuberant vegetation; and the cultivated part is peculiarly fertile.'

Shelley and his friend Thomas Peacock often walked when they wanted to go to London from Marlow. It was thirty-two miles to the Tyburn turnpike and after a night or two in London they would return the same way.

Shelley's contemporary, John Keats (1795–1821), went on a walking tour with his friend Charles Armitage Brown in 1818. Starting at Lancaster they went through the Lakes into Western Scotland as far as Cromarty. On the day they set out they got up at four o'clock in the morning. As it was raining they waited until seven o'clock before starting. Just as they left Lancaster a labourer was heard to comment: 'There go a couple of gentlemen. Having nothing to do, they're finding hard work for themselves.'

Originally the tour had been intended to take four months but Keats returned early by boat after some two months on account of ill health. He came back as brown as a berry but his shoes were almost worn away and his only jacket all torn. Brown and Keats averaged about twenty miles a day. Keats said he'd undertaken the tour because it would give him more experience, rid him of some of his prejudices, make him more used to hardship, and strengthen his reach in poetry.

Keats produced no poetry directly descriptive of the tour, but he did write poems that were inspired by particular incidents such as *To Ailsa, Ben Nevis* and *Lines Written in the Highlands After a Visit to Burn's Country*. Keats wrote to his friend Reynolds on the tour: 'I cannot write about scenery and visitings. Fancy is indeed less than present palpable reality, but it is greater than remembrance.'

When Keats lived at Hampstead he used to walk for an hour every day. It was on a Sunday walk that he composed *To Autumn. On First Looking into Chapman's Homer* was composed on an early morning walk from Clerkenwell to Poultry in October 1816.

When Keats walked through the nearby Kilburn Meadows with his friend Haydon he would repeat, or rather chant, his poetry. As a townsman he wrote:

> To one who has been long in city pent,
> 'Tis very sweet to look into the fair
> And open face of heaven, – to breath a prayer
> Full in the smile of the blue firmament.

The novelist and poet, Emily Brontë (1820–1849), who wrote the poem *Come walk with me* vividly describes her love of walking on the Yorkshire moors in *Wuthering Heights* as well as in her poetry. Her father was an active walker and encouraged his six children from an early age to walk out over the moors. They mainly used to walk upwards from Haworth Parsonage towards the 'purple-black' moors, seldom downward through the village. This had a deep influence on Emily's brilliant writing. Edward Thomas wrote of Emily: 'She fits into the moorland – she is part of it – like the curlew and the heather; and she herself knew it. The moorland was a necessity to her, but it was also her chief pleasure and joy.'

Charlotte Brontë speaking of her sister Emily and Haworth wrote:

> The scenery of these hills is not good; it is not romantic it is scarcely striking . . . it is only higher up, deep in amongst the ridges of the moors that imagination can find rest for the sole of her foot, and even if she finds it there, she must be a solitude – loving raven – no gentle dove . . .
> My Emily loved the moors . . . She found in the bleak solitude many and dear delights.

It was from Emily's experience of walking on these moors that *Wuthering Heights* became such a powerful and evocative novel.

The Dorset poet William Barnes (1801–1886) would walk sixteen to twenty-three miles on a Sunday to conduct a service when he became a cleric. The hire of transport on a Sunday in his time was so costly that there was every encouragement to walk. Even when he was eighty years old, Barnes was capable of walking twelve miles on a Sunday to conduct five services. He walked for pleasure as well as in the course of his work. In Barnes's earlier days when he had his school at Mere he used to take pupils on rambles of six or eight miles. He saw country walks as providing recreation as well as study. For himself it was a great source of inspiration for his poetry. A friend of William Barnes's daughter noted of Barnes: 'walks with him were always full of interest. We were walking round what to

commonplace people would have been a very prosy field, but in his hands the field became all poetry.'

Another country clergyman, Francis Kilvert (1840–1879), was forced to walk long distances going about his duties, visiting the sick, his congregation and friends because there was no alternative. However, he, like Barnes, also enjoyed walking for pleasure.

One of our greatest English novelists, Charles Dickens (1812–1870), enjoyed two styles of walking. One for the town, the other for the countryside. 'I am both a town traveller and a country traveller' he wrote 'always on the road.' His town walking he called his 'vagabond loitering walking.' He walked the London streets, noting the different kinds of street life, the way people lived and talked and carried on their affairs. He observed the filth, the congestion, the inadequate water supply leading to crime and disease. He heard the shrill voices of children who had no place to play but the refuse heaps of the streets.

Dickens's walks in the countryside were of a very different kind. These were undertaken to distract himself from the pressures of both his prolific writings and later the public readings from his books. Dickens always went on these country walks at a vigorous pace.

In August 1843 Dickens wrote to his friend and biographer John Forster from Broadstairs how the previous day had been one of terrific heat yet 'I performed an insane match against time of eighteen miles by the milestones in four and a half hours under a burning sun the whole way.' When staying in Italy he wrote to Forster about the bad weather in November, 'worse than any November English weather I have ever beheld or any weather I have had experience of anywhere.' Yet in sheer determination to get the better of such conditions, Dickens walked twelve miles in the mountain rain. Later that same month, after finishing his work, he walked fifteen miles to an inn for dinner.

In 1857 Dickens went walking in the Cumberland fells with Wilkie Collins. This was, Dickens said 'to escape from myself. I want to go anywhere – take any tour – see anything.' And so

Emily Brontë's 'chief pleasure and joy' – Haworth Moor.

the Cumberland fells were chosen as a relaxation after the exhaustion of writing and public readings. Dickens dragged Collins up Carrick Fell ('a gloomy old mountain 1,500 feet high'). They went up in 'a tremendous rain' with 'black mists' and lost their way. Collins sprained an ankle, leaping down a watercourse. Dickens had to carry him the rest of the way. Whilst Collins lay in their sitting-room for the next three days, Dickens feverishly roamed the countryside. 'A man who can do nothing by halves' Collins commented on Dickens.

The normal pattern of Dickens's life was to divide his day into work and exercise. When he was younger his exercise was riding or walking; later walking only. Dickens suffered from acute sleeplessness. He would get up soon after lying down, go out walking and return home at sunrise. 'My special feat was turning out of bed at two, after a hard day, pedestrian and otherwise, and walking thirty miles into the country for breakfast.'

Dickens himself wrote to Forster: 'I have now no relief but in action. I am incapable of rest. I am quite confident I should rust, break and die, if I spared myself. Much better to die, doing.' As he worked, so he walked, driving himself as fast as he possibly could. In 1864 although he had a swollen foot (probably gout), he regularly walked ten miles a day.

A walker who made a cult of vagabondage was George Borrow (1803–1881). The son of an army officer, who had risen from the ranks, George Borrow's earliest years were spent wandering about the country, often with gipsy friends. In his early twenties he took to the road 'travelling on foot ... leaving my subsequent movements to be determined by providence.' At the age of twenty-nine, when he was seeking a job with the British and Foreign Bible Society and had no money for the coach fare, he walked the 112-mile journey from Norwich to London in twenty-seven hours, spending fivepence halfpenny on the way. Later in life he made extensive tours (including much walking) of Wales (several times), Cornwall, Scotland, Ireland and the Isle of Man, always with a notebook in his hand. Only the tours of Wales were turned into a book, *Wild Wales*. Often he took his wife

and stepdaughter on tour but then left them whilst he went walking for several weeks. In 1854 Borrow went up Snowdon with his stepdaughter, Henrietta. No feminist, he was doubtful whether she would be able to manage the walk, but she did. They went up with a guide and had refreshments at the 'rude cabin' at the top. The journey up and back to Llanberis took four hours.

Borrow was very much an eccentric and an individualist. A tall well-built man, he was always physically active whether riding a horse, wielding an axe, walking or swimming. He generally liked being by himself; his view of the world was that of a solitary and romantic man. He liked talking to people he met by the wayside – gypsies, vagrants, labourers and even criminals especially in his early years; although in later years he was more respectable. He was always keen on his walks to visit antiquities, especially Celtic ones, and, as a versatile linguist, he was always very interested in the local language.

Both as a boy and a man George Meredith (1828–1909) considered hard exercise vital to one's physical well-being. When, as a young man, he lived in Ebury Street, Pimlico, he would walk to Esher in Surrey and back, covering some thirty or forty miles in a day. His friend H M Hyndman said of Meredith:

> He took a lot out of himself, not only intellectually but physically ... He was always throwing clubs about or going through gymnastic exercises or taking long walks at a great pace ... It was the same with his writing. He never pretended to take matters easily.

It was his intense temperament that sought release in excessive exercise. He always walked quickly. He never sauntered, he never lounged; an old friend commented, Meredith always strode like a giant.

For the last forty years of his life Meredith lived at Flint Cottage, Box Hill, Surrey, and he took long walks in the surrounding countryside. From these he stored up many impressions of nature and scenery which found expression in his novels and poems. 'A rapid walker' he wrote in *The Egoist*

The Galloway Hills were John Buchan's choice for a marathon hike
'in the teeth of the wind with rain in his face . . .'

'poetically minded gathers multitudes of images on his way.' Walking with nature as his companion remained Meredith's passion until he contracted locomotor ataxia, a malady of the spine, which severely limited his walking. 'I can't walk any of my old strides' he wrote to Robert Louis Stevenson in 1880. Later the malady crippled him completely.

Walkers are frequently portrayed in Meredith's novels. One of those was Vernon Whitford in *The Egoist*, a character based on Meredith's friend, Leslie Stephen (1832–1904). Meredith described Whitford as 'a lean long-walker and scholar' and 'a Phoebus Apollo turned fasting friar' who 'attacked the dream-giving earth with tremendous long strides that his blood might be lively at the throne of understanding.'

Meredith was a sort of ex officio member of the Sunday Tramps, a rambling club founded by Leslie Stephen in 1879, the year in which *The Egoist* was first published. Stephen first organized a few friends, for the most part addicted to philosophy, to take long Sunday walks. Later the group was expanded to include many well-known intellectuals. The members included Croom Robertson, Walter Pollock, F W Maitland, Robert Bridges, R B Haldane (later Lord Haldane[1]), Lord Justice Romer, Sir Fredrich Pollock, Sir Herbert Stephen, John Collier, Cotter Morison and I MacColl. There were no women members.

The Sunday Tramps existed for fifteen years and walks were organized every other Sunday from October to June in Surrey, Kent and Hertfordshire. There were never more than about twenty effective members but if ten took part it was considered a good number.

The Tramps were entertained at various times by George Meredith and Charles Darwin. Meredith would join the Tramps when he was going to entertain them after the walk. Meredith said that a shorthand writer in attendance on the Tramps would have been a benefactor to the country. The view of F W Maitland, one of the Tramps, on this remark of Meredith's was 'the occasions on which a shorthand writer was desirable coincided somewhat exactly with those on which Mr Meredith honoured us with his company.' Meredith was very much a talkative walker.

Leslie Stephen, when a tutor at Cambridge, was president of a walking society, the Boa Constrictor Club. He was nick-named 'The Old Serpent' and organized undergraduates on weekly walks. Stephen won the mile race at Cambridge University, was an enthusiastic oarsman, a rowing coach and one of the earliest Alpine climbers. (Previous to the mid-nineteenth century the Alps had been something to marvel at from a distance, not something to climb.) Stephen was most at his ease, his biographer F W Maitland noted, when his legs were moving fast. In *The Egoist* 'Have you walked far to-day?' Miss Middleton asked of Mr Whitford. 'Nine and a half hours … I had to walk off my temper' came the reply. Stephen once walked from Cambridge to London, fifty miles, in twelve hours to attend a dinner.

Stephen was portrayed by his daughter, Virginia Woolf, as Mr Ramsey in her novel *To The Lighthouse*. One of the characters, William Bankes, when he thought of Ramsey imagined him 'skidding along a road, himself hung around with that solitude which seemed to be his natural air.' Ramsey himself recalls when a boy he had walked about the country with nothing but a biscuit in his pocket. Wistfully, in his later years, he remembered walking all day, with a meal of bread and cheese in a pub.

> That was the country he liked best, over there, those sandhills dwindling away into darkness. One could walk all day without meeting a soul. There was not a house scarcely, not a single village for miles on end. One could worry things out alone. There were little sandy beaches where no one had been since the beginning of time.

Another writer who was encouraged in his writings in turn by Leslie Stephen and George Meredith was Robert Louis Stevenson (1850–1894). Throughout his life he was dogged by

---

[1] Haldane in his younger days at the Bar, used to take a Saturday evening train to Brighton and walk the fifty-odd miles back to London on the Sunday.

ill-health. 'I have spent nearly all my life in expectation of death' was how he described it. He suffered from a chronic bronchial condition (probably tuberculosis). In his late twenties, while he was still fit enough, he did a lot of walking. He walked in the Pentland Hills near Edinburgh, near Bridge of Allan on the fringe of the Highlands and in the Chilterns. He took a keen interest in sports and athletic activities including swimming, skating, sailing and canoeing. Most of his poetry is written about the open air even though much of it was composed in bed.

> For my part [he wrote] I travel not to go anywhere but to go. I travel for travel's sake. The great affair is to move, to feel the needs and hitches of our life more nearly, to come off this feather bed of civilization, and find the globe granite underfoot and strewn with cutting flints.

His writing has a spirit of adventure and a bubbling enthusiasm, an exuberance that covered his determination not to complain too much of his weak constitution.

Richard Jefferies (1848–1887), a contemporary of Stevenson, also suffered from ill-health. He had not the physical strength for long-distance walking but walked in the localities near where he lived and worked as a journalist, in Wiltshire, Sussex and Surrey. 'I want to be always in company with the sun and sea and earth' he wrote. 'These and the stars by night are my natural companions.' Jefferies repeated his walks again and again. In those walks he escaped from 'the constant routine of house-life, the same work, the same thought in the work, the little circumstances regularly recurring which will dull the edge of thought.' Although loving the country, and delighting in nature, of which he was a very astute and detailed observer, Jefferies was also fond of London.

> I am very fond of what I may call a thickness of the people such as exists in London ... I dream in London as much as in the woodlands ... I like the solitude of the hills and the hum of the crowded city; I dislike the little towns and villages.

Jefferies, though a mystic and naturalist, firmly believed in physical exercise:

> I believe – I do more than think – I believe it to be a sacred duty incumbent upon every one, man and woman, to add to and encourage their physical life, by exercise and in every manner ... those who stunt their physical life are most certainly stunting their souls.

In her memoirs, Nadezhda Krupskaya (1869–1939), tells how in their years of exile in various European countries she and her husband Lenin were avid walkers. Whilst in London in 1902–3 they explored various parts of London on foot. They enjoyed, Krupskaya records

> ... the quiet squares, the detached houses, with their separate entrances and shining windows adorned with greenery ... but tucked away nearby were the mean little streets, inhabited by the London working people, where lines with washing hung across the street and pale children played in the gutter.

Lenin and Krupskaya visited open-air markets, illuminated by flares, on a pay-day evening. They went into public houses and attended church services and were very impressed by the numerous free reading rooms. One of their favourite places for a walk was Primrose Hill. Krupskaya commented:

> Nearly the whole of London could be seen from the hill – a vast smoke-wreathed city receding into the distance. From here we got close to nature, penetrating deep into the parks and along green paths.

A writer who made his name by writing about walking was Hilaire Belloc (1870–1953). In 1901 he made up his mind to walk from Toul in France, where he had done his military service, to Rome. His route was to be a straight line as far as practicable. His original plan was to sleep in the open, without a tent or sleeping bag, but he found this was not workable in practice. Indeed he did not carry much more equipment than

Edward Thomas would often escape from his all-consuming melancholy
to the banks of a Welsh upland stream.

Demelza's Cove in Cornwall – a county extensively explored by the consummate vagabond, George Borrow.

Wordsworth and his friend Jones when they went to France a century earlier.

Previously, when twenty years old, Belloc had taken three months to cross the United States, mainly on foot, selling rough sketches of the landscape to get money for board and lodging. The object of his journey was to persuade Elodie Hogan to marry him. Belloc's tramping was in vain. He was refused. Some five years later he was accepted. Like many undergraduates of his time Belloc thought nothing of walking the fifty-four miles from Oxford to London. On one occasion he covered the distance in eleven and a half hours.

Belloc wrote about many parts of England, but especially Sussex where he had his home for nearly fifty years.

> The great hills of the South Country
> They stand along the sea:
> And it's there walking in the high woods
> That I could wish to be,
> And the men that were boys when I was a boy
> Walking along with me.

The vagabond tradition was revived by W H Davies (1871–1940). He had been a real tramp at the time of the great immigration to the United States when the country was swarming with tramps. His famous book, *Autobiography of a Super-tramp*, first published in 1908, had a wide sale both in this country and in America. Davies lost a leg whilst jumping a train and as he could not afford a metal limb, he was fitted with a wooden stump. This, however, did not prevent him continuing his long walks. His poetry, direct and easy to understand, expresses the joys and the hazards of the life of the vagrant.

A contemporary writer of Davies, who was an enthusiastic walker but was certainly not in the vagabond tradition, was John Buchan (1875–1940), the Scottish novelist and bi-ographer of Walter Scott. 'Wood sea and hill were the intimacies of my childhood' he wrote 'and they have never lost their spell for me … The Border Hills were my own possession in which my roots went deep.' At school he had a six-mile walk each day having to arrive at eight o'clock in the morning. No doubt many of his contemporaries had similar experiences. He was accustomed to sleep out of doors in any weather including December frosts. He once walked sixty-three miles on end in the Galloway Hills. He wrote with delight of a long tramp in the teeth of the wind with rain in his face and a mist swirling down the glens. His wife told how he would go up a hillside like lightning and walk nearly every companion to a standstill. It was this experience of the open-air life that enabled him to give so much background to the fifty books he wrote in his spare time whilst pursuing an active career in publishing, politics as an M P and diplomacy as Governor-General of Canada.

John Masefield (1878–1967) was greatly influenced in his early years by and was a personal friend of W B Yeats. Throughout his life Masefield composed, whenever he could out of doors. In his youth he went on long solitary walks of exploration in London. On holiday in Devon he undertook twenty-five-mile walks with Jack Yeats, an artist and the poet's brother. More usually Masefield's walks were shorter, near where he was living at the time: Epping Forest; Hampstead Heath; at Wallingford on the downs with Rupert Brooke; at Boar's Hill near Oxford. He felt a strong kinship with George Borrow both as a vagabond writer and teller of a good tale. When Masefield became a success and was lionized, he never disowned his early vagabonding days and the sympathy it gave him with the down and out.

A man with whom Masefield had a lot of sympathy and to whom he gave encouragement was John Millington Synge (1871–1909). From his boyhood his great recreation was going on long walks whether in the countryside and hills around Dublin, the Bogs of West Kerry and Connemara or the German mountains. Long and regular walks played an important part in his long courtship with Molly Allgood, one of the actresses in the Abbey Theatre. The courtship never ended in marriage, perhaps because of his early death. For five years, Synge's writing career, on which he was determined, met with no success. He could get nothing published. Yeats who had been to the Aran Islands for material for his projected but never finished novel, *The Speckled Bird*, suggested Synge should go there to collect material for his writing. Synge went and spent a total of four and a half summer months on the Islands in each of the years 1898–1902. He went walking round the three islands, talking to, listening to and living with the people of Aran. His writings became transformed. An entirely new art was created. The bilingual man and woman of Aran became Synge's hallmark. A man of no obvious talent became a writer of genius.

Helen Thomas, wife of the poet Edward Thomas (1878–1917), told how her husband's greatest pleasure, and certainly his greatest need, was to walk and be alone. His most satisfying days were when he wandered far afield alone over forgotten footpaths and hidden lanes, stopping at remote and primitive inns. Walking for him was not merely the joy of exercise – he swung along with a long slow stride – but, as a nature lover, he would observe the birds and flowers and clouds and all the life of the hedges and copses, the beauty of the contours of the hills and the symmetry of the trees. All this experience he was able to transcribe into words, first in prose and, in his later years, into poetry.

Helen has told how her husband suffered from severe depressions. Sometimes his broody melancholy would shut her out in a lonely exile and he would go out and walk all night and only return in the morning. 'Perhaps from the silence of the night and from the natural sounds of early dawn,' wrote Helen in her autobiography, 'and from the peace of solitude and the beauty of intangible things he would find healing and calm.' He walked, for the most part alone, over a great part of southern England and southern Wales.

> By the English country his soul was revived when it was faint with despair, and comforted as some are by religion or music. [wrote Helen.] Solitary on the bare downs, or in the sheltered valleys, on the ancient tracks above which the kestrel has always circled and hovered, and where the sheep have nibbled for such ages that the very grass and flowers have adapted their growth to evade the ceaseless menace of

their teeth; or leaning over a gate to talk to the ploughman who, with such skilful ease, swings his plough at the end of the furrow; or wandering among the epitaphed tombstones of the village churchyard; or sitting by a stream reading Traherne or Chaucer, or in the evening at the inn, or anywhere where the rural life of England continued in the traditional ways – there he could throw off his melancholy brooding and be content.

Edward Thomas's love of the open air and of the tradition and history and life of the English country was so strong in him that before comfort and ease and security he chose to live away from towns. There he could walk all day without touching a road except to cross it; 'where the Pilgrim's Way would become as familiar as his native suburban street; where notebook after notebook would be filled with records of beauty and wonder and events of interest.'

Another First World War poet was Ivor Gurney (1890–1937). He was a song writer, and composer of chamber and piano music and orchestral works as well as a poet. Sir John Squire wrote:

> I have known composers with a fine literary sense and poets who have loved music but neither compose nor play. I have known no man save Gurney who had the double creative gift that Rossetti had in his two arts.

Gurney was in the vagabond tradition, he thought nothing of walking from London to Gloucester, sleeping out in barns or under hedgerows when the weather was good, earning a few pence by singing folks songs in country inns; carrying little more than his pipe and tobacco pouch, pencils and notebooks, he jotted down music or poetry as it occurred to him. He walked very much in his native county of Gloucestershire. He set some of Edward Thomas's songs to music.

Author of more than a hundred books on politics, economics, biography, labour and socialist history and jointly with his wife, Margaret, of detective novels, G D H Cole (1889–1959), walked regularly as a relaxation in his earlier years. Although not a robust person he walked fast and hard and faster and harder uphill or over rough ground. He and his wife made frequent walking tours of William Morris's Cotswolds, William Cobbett's southern counties and the villages and byways of Sussex. They covered nearly all the ground which Cobbett had ridden on horseback a hundred years before. Cole wrote a biography of Cobbett and produced a new edition of *Rural Rides* with maps and biographical notes. Margaret was Cole's main walking companion but he did some walking tours with his former pupil at Oxford, Hugh Gaitskell, who had previously considered walking as a tiresome chore. Cole induced Gaitskell to discover the Cotswolds by footpath and Ordnance Survey map and to appreciate how much history could be found in southern England simply by walking in it.

When a student at Oxford W H Auden (1907–1973) was fond of taking extremely long walks – especially after he was medically advised not to do so because of his flat feet. He was always an individualist. Auden had a fast stride which made it difficult for his friends to keep up with him and he was not prepared to accommodate his walking companions by adjusting to their pace. His favourite walk was along the side of the canal by the gasworks and the municipal rubbish dump which he thought the most beautiful walk in Oxford. He was not really interested in nature unless nature was at work reclaiming old mines or derelict machinery. Auden disliked Wordsworth and his approach to nature.

Bernard Levin, the well-known journalist and music critic, is a modern follower of Charles Lamb in that he particularly likes urban walks. He takes the train to some outer suburbs and then walks all the way to Marble Arch down 'that almost Roman-straight diagonal that eventually becomes the homely Edgware Road'; or from Epping Forest via the City to Central London. His favourite walk consists of walking back and forth across the Thames in London, crossing every pedestrian bridge from Tower to Hammersmith, a total of sixteen walkable bridges and some fourteen miles in distance. In his recent book *Enthusiasms* he finds that thoughts when walking are positive, life-filled, confident and serene whereas thoughts at home on the same subject are likely to lead to doubt, fear and negativity. He urges that the feeling of being tired while a walk is in progress has to be kept at bay otherwise the walk will cease to be a pleasure; walking, he strongly feels, should only be undertaken as a pleasure.

A contemporary novelist and travel writer, Paul Theroux, spent three months in 1982 travelling round the coast of Britain, partly by train and partly walking. He was an American who had lived in London for eleven years but had seldom been outside the capital during that time. As a foreigner he could see things with a different eye. He found much of the British coast to be empty. Things that were dangerous (like nuclear power stations) or that stank (like sewage farms) were shoved on to the coast. He found the coast a natural home for oil refineries and gas storage tanks and more rubbish on the coast than in any inland dump. The coast was laden with car-parks, junk yards, gun emplacements, military installations and radar dishes, American missile bases and squads of American marines in various coves. He thought great parts of the country were being turned into what they were before the railway age. Villages were becoming crabbed and shrunken as businesses and facilities closed; people who stayed in rural areas were becoming more and more tied to their houses. Parts of Britain which for hundreds of years had been frequented by travellers had now become inaccessible.

What Theroux did like, however, in Britain were things such as the bread, the fish, the cheese, the flower gardens, the apples, the clouds, the newspapers, the beer, the woollen cloth, the radio programmes, the parks, the Indian restaurants, the amateur dramatics, the postal service, the fresh vegetables, the trains and the modesty and truthfulness of the people.

The most well-known English contemporary walker is John Hillaby. He has walked from Land's End to John O'Groats, a journey of some 1,100 miles which was accomplished in fifty-five walking days. He carried a tent to give himself independence but did not hesitate to put up at a hotel or pub when convenient. Before he started the walk he trained for three months. A few years later Hillaby did another long walk from the North Sea to the Mediterranean by way of the Alps. This was much the same distance as the walk through Britain and took two months. He spent six months working out the route and seeking information from various sources.

In his walk through Britain Hillaby found the main obstacles were mist and impenetrable cloud, the deep bogs of Dartmoor, the difficulty of finding food in Wales on a Sunday and in the more isolated parts of Scotland, sometimes difficulty in obtaining a bath and, on occasions, being cut off by flood. Always ready to stop and talk on his journey, Hillaby was fascinated by the varying accents and dialects of the different parts of the country. By the end he felt the mosaic of his own country and its people had become a sensible pattern. In all his books Hillaby shows a zest for life, he is interested in what goes on around him, he has a good knowledge of local history. He says he likes to peel off the miles; there is a dragon-slaying feeling in covering distance.

In the Romantic period it is noteworthy that the male writers walked with females. William Wordsworth walked with his sister Dorothy, his wife Mary and his daughter Dora. Shelley walked with his wife Mary and her half-sister Claire. Lamb walked with his sister Mary and later his adopted daughter, Emma Isola. In the rest of the nineteenth century it is significant that there is no mention of men walking with women. The Sunday Tramps were all male. Pictures of walking clubs in the latter half of the nineteenth century seem to be all male. So far as is known, the tramp vogue of the early twentieth century was an all-male effort and it would be difficult to name a woman who has taken up the vagabond cult. By the twentieth century however walking habits were beginning to change. Lenin walked regularly with his wife Krupskaya; Edward Thomas with his wife Helen Thomas; D H Lawrence walked with Jessie Chambers and his other women friends. In modern times, in this country, it would be unthinkable to have a single-sex rambling club.

Have things changed since Hazlitt in 1821 wrote his famous essay *On Going A Journey*? At the time a 'journey' meant walking. In Hazlitt's time there were not so many alternative forms of travel as there are today. If anyone today wrote *On Going A Journey* it would be assumed that at least part of the journey would be on wheels. As a paean of walking for a day on one's own Hazlitt's essay is as meaningful today as when it was written.

Walking is one of the simplest and most primitive forms of recreation; no equipment is required for a day's walk. For longer periods some equipment and preparation become important. Walking can be enjoyed as a time for contemplation by the lone walker or as a social occasion for those who prefer to walk in company. Walking is not competitive; it can be practised in the town, in the country, beside the sea, on the hills or in the mountains; by day or by night, in almost any weather and in all seasons.

Looking into the future, whatever technological changes there may be, fundamentally walking is for ever, as many of the extracts in the following anthology clearly illustrate.

DONALD VEALL

BIOGRAPHIES

MAX BEERBOHM (1872–1956)

Born in London, educated at Charterhouse and Merton College, Oxford. Caricaturist, writer, dandy and wit. His sophisticated drawings and parodies were mainly of his famous and fashionable contemporaries. He parodied the literary styles of Henry James, Wells and Kipling among others. He was dramatic critic of *Saturday Review* from 1898 to 1912, succeeding Shaw. In 1910 he settled in Italy except for the periods of the two World Wars.

WILFRID SCAWEN BLUNT (1840–1922)

An explorer, horseman, horse-breeder, shot, sculptor, painter, prose writer, social diarist and poet. He was strongly anti-imperialist, especially on Egypt and Ireland. He was in the diplomatic service for a while, but this was not his media, he was essentially 'wild as a hawk.' He himself said he was fortunate he did not have to work for a living.

GEORGE BORROW (1803–1881)

Born at East Dereham, Norfolk. He had a nomadic boyhood as his father was in the army and George moved around with his father's regiment. Consequently he was educated at many different places: Huddersfield, Edinburgh, Clonmel and Norwich. He was articled to a solicitor but did not take up law as a career. Instead he adopted literature as a profession. He travelled extensively in Great Britain, France, Germany, Russia and the East, studying the languages of the countries he visited. In Russia and Spain he acted as agent for the British and Foreign Bible Society. He wrote a number of books based on his experiences and travels, generally written some twenty years after the event. It is difficult to distinguish the facts from the fiction in his books. *The Bible in Spain* (1834) was an immediate success and something like a 'best-seller'. *Lavengro* (1851) and *The Romany Rye* (1857) at first attracted no interest. It was some fifty years later, after Borrow's death, that these two books became popular when vagabondage walking became an acceptable cult.

ROBERT BRIDGES (1844–1930)

He was educated at Eton and Corpus Christi College, Oxford. He began in childhood to have a fondness for long walks through the countryside which were to form the basis of many of the ideas incorporated in his poetry. He qualified as a doctor and practised as a house physician at St Bartholomew's Hospital and later at the Hospital for Sick Children, Great Ormand Street. He gave up medicine after a bout of ill-health in 1881 and devoted himself to writing. For the rest of his life he lived near Oxford, first at Yattendon in Berkshire and then at Boar's Hill. In those places he could walk, mostly alone, along the footpaths around Oxford. He was made Poet Laureate in 1913. Bridges is mainly known for his lyrical poetry, *The Testament of Beauty* (a long poem on his spiritual philosophy), his anthology of prose and verse, *The Spirit of Man*, and for rescuing the poetry of Gerard Manley Hopkins from obscurity.

ANNE BRONTË (1820–1849).

Born at Thornton, Yorkshire, she was the youngest of the Brontë sisters. Her simple hymn-like poems reveal her religious preoccupation. Her two novels *Agnes Grey* and *The Tenant of Wildfell Hall* are less well known than those of her more talented sisters but have some admirers. George Moore thought *Agnes Grey* 'simple and beautiful as a muslin dress.'

EMILY BRONTË (1818–1849).

Emily, born at Thornton, Yorkshire, was the fifth child, two older sisters died young. The family moved to Haworth in 1820. Emily spent most of her life at Haworth and was much involved in the domestic chores of the parsonage. When she was away from Haworth at school and then as governess she was never really happy. The Brontë children, brought up mainly in the isolation of the Haworth parsonage, were very much left to themselves. The moors with their changes of weather and seasons were their playground. The genius of Emily as illustrated in her poetry and in the novel *Wuthering Heights* was not appreciated until long after her death.

ROBERT BURNS (1759–1796).

Born at Alloway, Ayrshire, the son of an impoverished farmer. The suffering which he saw his father undergo made him a rebel against the social order of the day. He became a tenant farmer and published his first book of poems in 1786. This was an immediate success and thereafter he led a dual life as tenant farmer at Mossgiel and Ellisland and literary lion. In later life he was able to give up farming and he became an exciseman at Dunfries. Burns has become the national poet of Scotland, celebrated annually with rites associated with no other man of letters in any other country. It is through his many songs set to old Scottish airs that Burns has become known the world over. It was Burns's ability to speak with the great anonymous voice of the Scottish people that has aroused so great a following for him. He composed much of his poetry with a tune in his head whilst either walking or riding.

WILKIE COLLINS (1824–1889).

Born in London, he was the son of William Collins, the landscape painter. Whilst still a schoolboy Wilkie developed a gift for inventing mystery tales. He was put into the tea trade but disliked it; he studied law at Lincoln's Inn and was called to the Bar, but did not like the law either. As a writer he was the first English novelist to write mystery stories. His most well-known works are *The Woman in White* and *The Moonstone*. He was a close friend of Charles Dickens and they each exercised a considerable influence on the other's

writing. In 1850, before the railway came to Cornwall, Wilkie Collins went on a walking tour of that county with an artist friend and wrote a book describing their experiences.

WILLIAM HENRY DAVIES (1871–1940).

Born at Newport, Monmouthshire. Davies insisted he was neither Welsh or English but an ancient Briton belonging to the Silurian tribe. Nature poet and author of *Autobiography of a Super-tramp*. After serving as an apprentice to a picture framer, he went to America at the age of twenty-two and led a vagrant life there. Subsequently he returned to England. He was a friend of Edward Thomas, who gave him much support and encouragement. The simplicity of Davies's lyrics distinguishes him from that of his Georgian contemporaries.

CHARLES DICKENS (1812–1870).

Born in Portsmouth, the son of a government clerk. He received little formal education. After being a solicitor's clerk, he became a reporter of debates in the House of Commons and wrote for various periodicals. In April 1836 he began the publication of *Pickwick Papers* in twenty monthly instalments. This gave him success and financial ease. He travelled widely: to USA twice, Italy, and Switzerland. He was founder and, for a short time, editor of the *Daily News*. He founded the weekly periodical *Household Words* (succeeded in 1859 by *All the Year Round*) in which were published much of his later writings. Tolstoy said of Dickens '. . . all his characters are my personal friends.'

ELEANOR FARJEON (1881–1965).

Granddaughter of Joseph Jefferson, the celebrated American actor. Born in London, her parents' home at Hampstead was a meeting place for actors, writers and musicians. Her father was a prolific Victorian novelist. Eleanor had no formal education. She was friendly with Edward and Helen Thomas. She wrote children's stories, short stories, poetry, a book on Edward Thomas's last years and collaborated with her brother Herbert on plays and an operetta.

JAMES ELROY FLECKER (1884–1915).

Educated at Uppingham and Trinity College, Oxford. He studied Oriental languages at Cambridge. In 1910 he went to Constantinople in the Consular Service. The rest of his life was spent mainly in the east with intervals in England. In 1913 he was obliged to go to Switzerland because of his health. He died of tuberculosis at Davos. He published several collections of verse. The work for which he is best remembered is the poetic Eastern play *Hassan*.

IVOR GURNEY (1890–1937).

Born in Gloucester, the son of a tailor. He attended at the Royal College of Music. He volunteered at the outbreak of the First World War, served as a private on the Western Front from 1915 to 1917 and was wounded and gassed. From 1922 until his death he was confined to a mental hospital and eventually died of consumption. He composed nearly three hundred songs. With the passage of time his poetry has gained in appreciation.

THOMAS HARDY (1840–1928).

Born at Upper Bockhampton, near Dorchester, the son of a builder. Hardy qualified as an architect and practised in London, Dorchester and Weymouth. After having his second novel published, Hardy gave up architecture for writing. His first successful novel, *Far from the Madding Crowd*, was published in 1874. Hardy himself classified his novels into three groups, those of character and environment, romances and fantasies and novels of ingenuity. It is the first group on which his reputation as a novelist is based. He had a profound knowledge of the speech customs and way of life in what Hardy called 'Wessex'. In his novels he was an innovator and wrote frankly about sexual problems in *Tess of the D'Urbervilles* and *Jude the Obscure*. Hardy gave up novel writing after the appearance of the latter book because of the savage treatment it received from reviewers who were upset by Hardy's frankness. From that time onwards Hardy concentrated on poetry. This took many forms: narrative, dramatic, philosophic, elegiac and literary. Hardy attached more importance to his poetry than his novels.

WILLIAM HAZLITT (1778–1830).

He was born at Maidstone, Kent, the son of a Unitarian minister. Most of his youth was spent in the village of Wem near Shrewsbury. At first he showed an inclination for painting, but he soon gave this up for literature. He was friendly with many of the men of letters of his time, including Lamb, Wordsworth and Coleridge. He wrote and lectured on many subjects, including drama, art, travel and literary criticism.

GERARD MANLEY HOPKINS (1844–1889).

Born at Stratford, Essex, and educated at Highgate School and Balliol College, Oxford. He was a pupil of Jowett and Pater. He became a Roman Catholic convert and was ordained into the Roman Catholic priesthood. In 1884 he was appointed to the chair of Greek at Dublin University. His poems, none of which was published in his lifetime, were collected by his friend Robert Bridges. The first collected poems were not published until twenty-nine years after his death. He was a poet of much originality and a skilful innovator in rhythm which had a considerable influence on later poets.

WILLIAM HENRY HUDSON (1841–1922).

Born of American parents of English descent near Buenos Aires. Much of his youth was spent roaming the pampas where his father had a sheep farm. He came to England in 1869 and became a naturalized British subject in 1900. He suffered from ill-health but from his earliest years he was a sympathetic and patient observer of nature, particularly birds. His nature books are amongst the best ever written. He wandered either on foot or on cycle over many of the counties of England studying his birds and insects; he was especially fond of Sussex, Wiltshire (which reminded him of the Argentine) and above all Hampshire.

RICHARD JEFFERIES (1848–1887).

Son of a small farmer, he was first a reporter on a local paper and then a freelance journalist. He spent nearly twenty-nine years in the neighbourhood of Coate, Wiltshire. He also lived at Surbiton and Brighton. He spent much of his time walking on the Wiltshire downs and in the Surrey and Sussex countryside. All was closely and truthfully observed by a naturalist of rare perception. He was naturally solitary, reserved and much given to meditation, he also liked the spectacle of humanity. Jefferies never enjoyed good health and he died at the early age of thirty-eight, the last five years being marred by intermittent illness and pain.

JOHN KEATS (1795–1821).

The son of a livery-stable keeper in Moorfields, London. He was apprenticed to an apothecary, but his indentures were cancelled so that he could qualify as a surgeon. He qualified but did not practise because he wanted to devote himself to writing. His poetry was savagely criticized in the current literary magazines. He was described as 'an ambitious apothecary's apprentice' whom the critic recommended should return to his pills and plasters. His true genius was only recognized slowly and posthumously. He was dogged by ill-health and left for Italy in 1820 only to die of consumption a few months later in Rome at the tragically early age of twenty-six.

FRANCIS KILVERT (1840–1879).

Born in Hardenhuish, Wiltshire, diarist of life in the English countryside in mid-Victorian times. A country clergyman in Radnorshire, Wiltshire and Herefordshire, He kept a diary from 1870 until his death, but had no intention of publishing it. A selection from the diary was first published in three volumes in 1938–1940 by the poet William Plomer.

CHARLES LAMB (1775–1834).

Born in London, the son of a scrivener, he lived there until 1823. Later he lived at Islington, Enfield and Edmonton. Essayist, literary critic and a great letter writer. He was educated at Christ's Hospital (then in London) where he formed an enduring friendship with Coleridge. He was employed as a clerk in the East India House from 1792–1825. In 1796 his sister Mary murdered their mother. Mary was never prosecuted. Charles agreed to accept responsibility for her for the rest of his life. Mary was confined to an asylum from time to time. Lamb is best remembered for his essays and his *Tales from Shakespeare* written jointly with Mary. His various homes were a meeting place for many of his well-known literary contemporaries.

DAVID HERBERT LAWRENCE (1885–1930).

Born at Eastwood, Nottinghamshire, the son of a miner. He was educated at University College, Nottingham. He was a schoolmaster before taking up writing as a profession. Apart from the years in England during the First World War, Lawrence and his wife, Frieda, lived mostly abroad in Italy, Sicily, Sardinia, Australia and New Mexico. He continually fought against ill-health. His novel, *The Rainbow*, completed in 1915 was supressed. He could not find a publisher for *Women in Love* completed in 1916. *Lady Chatterley's Lover* first published in 1928 was banned in several countries. He was one of the great English novelists of the twentieth century whose true genius was not recognized until after his death. He had several volumes of poems published, wrote travel books, short stories, plays, essay translations and letters; he also painted. He is portrayed as Mark Rampian in Aldous Huxley's *Point Counter Point*. In his younger days he was a keen walker, usually accompanied by one or more friends. He went on walking tours in the Alps, in Switzerland, and the Lake District.

GEORGE MEREDITH (1828–1909).

He was the grandson of Melchizedeh Meredity, a prosperous tailor and naval outfitter of Portsmouth. He was educated privately. In London after being articled to a solicitor, he turned to journalism. His first book of poems was published in

1851. His first important novel, *The Ordeal of Richard Feverel*, appeared in 1859, but sales were poor. He was not really successful as a novelist until *Diana of the Crossways* was published in 1885 after serial issue in *Fortnightly*. He was essentially a Londoner's writer. He loved the social life of London and the joys of getting out of the town and walking into Hampshire, Surrey, Kent and Sussex.

JOHN COWPER POWYS (1872–1963).
Born at Shirley, Derbyshire. Author and poet, brother of Llewellyn Powys, the essayist and novelist, and of Theodore Francis Powys, the novelist. He was a university extension lecturer for over forty years, spending many of them in the USA. He began his literary career as a poet, but he is chiefly known for his long novels. He also published many volumes of literary criticism and social philosophy. Always a great walker, John was the eldest child of a large family, most of whom enjoyed walking having been introduced to it by their father the Reverend Charles Powys.

PERCY BYSSHE SHELLEY (1792–1822).
Born near Horsham, Sussex, educated at Eton and sent down from Oxford University for publishing a pamphlet called *The Necessity of Atheism*. He lived at Keswick, various parts of London, Bath, Tremadoc in Wales, Marlow and near Windsor among other places before leaving for Italy for health reasons in 1818 where he led a wandering life. Although it is as a poet that Shelley is best known, he possessed great ability as a writer in many other spheres as essayist, dramatist, pamphleteer, translator in six languages, reviewer and letter writer. He was one of the greatest, and, in his lifetime, the most controversial of English Romantic thinkers and poets. All his life he loved boats but never learnt to swim and was drowned in a storm between Leghorn and Lerici, Italy.

EDWARD THOMAS (1878–1917).
Born in London of Welsh parents. He wrote biographical and topographical works and was one of the few poets who did not start to write poetry at an early age, starting when he was thirty-six, mainly at the suggestion of his friend the American poet, Robert Frost. Thomas was a great admirer of Richard Jefferies. A restless roving spirit, most of his poetry is about the English countryside which he knew so well because of his love of walking. His reputation has grown with the passing of the years. He never saw a poem published under his own name, just two or three under a pseudonym 'Edward Eastaway.' Thomas was killed in Flanders in the First World War.

GEORGE MACAULAY TREVELYAN (1876–1962).
Born at Welcombe near Stratford-on-Avon. Son of George Otto Trevelyan, historian and Cabinet Minister, and great nephew of Thomas Babington Macaulay. Educated at Harrow and Cambridge. A historian who believed that the writing of history was part of a nation's literary heritage. He and his wife did a lot of walking and cycling, visiting historical sites about which Trevelyan wrote. He particularly loved mountain walking and he climbed mountains in nearly every European country. North-East England was the part of England that he loved most to walk.

ELLEN WEETON (1776–?).
From humble and obscure origins, what little is known of her is told in *Journal of a Governess* published in 1936 and 1939.

VIRGINIA WOOLF (1882–1941).
Born near Rodwell, Sussex. Novelist, short-story writer and critic. She was educated at home by her father, Leslie Stephen. In 1904 she moved to Gordon Square, London, which later became the centre of the Bloomsbury Group. She married Leonard Woolf and later they founded together the Hogarth Press. After the First World War she started to experiment with novel writing. In her novels she wanted to stress the continuous flow of experience, the indefinability of character and external circumstances as they impinge on a character. This is shown in her unusual book *The Waves*. She experien-

ced mental collapses in her early years, recovered but finally committed suicide by drowning.

DOROTHY WORDSWORTH (1771–1855).

Born at Cockermouth, Cumberland. The only sister of William Wordsworth. From 1795 she was William's indispensable housekeeper and companion and remained with him for the rest of her life. She shared her brother's poetic ideals and aspirations and his delight in nature. From 1829 until her death she was an invalid; in 1835 sclerosis set in and her mind was affected.

WILLIAM WORDSWORTH (1770–1850).

Born at Cockermouth, Cumberland. He was the son of attorney and agent to Sir James Lowther (later Earl of Lonsdale) and was educated at the grammar school at Hawkshead. He went to St John's College, Cambridge, but did not take an honours degree. He lived for a year in France; later he lived at Racedown in Dorset, Alfoxden in Somerset, in Germany, Sockburn-on-Tees in Durham and finally settled at Grasmere in 1790 for the remainder of his life. Throughout his life he went on numerous tours, much of the time spent walking; he toured Scotland, Switzerland, Italy and other parts of Europe. In 1813 he was appointed Distributor of Stamps for Westmorland and part of Cumberland. He was made Poet Laureate in 1843.

'The huge and majestic form of St Paul's . . . the elegant line of the curve of Ludgate Hill.'

LITERARY WALKS

OF BRITAIN

LONDON

CITY OF LONDON

I left Coleridge at seven o'clock on Sunday morning, and walked towards the city in a very thoughtful and melancholy state of mind. I had passed through Temple Bar and by St. Dunstan's, noticing nothing, and entirely occupied with my own thoughts, when, looking up, I saw before me the avenue of Fleet Street, silent, empty and pure white, with a sprinkling of new-fallen snow, not a cart or carriage to obstruct the view, no noise, only a few soundless and dusky foot-passengers here and there. You remember the elegant line of the curve of Ludgate Hill, in which this avenue would terminate, and beyond, towering above it, was the huge and majestic form of St. Paul's, solemnised by a thin veil of falling snow. I cannot say how much I was affected at this unthought-of sight in such a place, and what blessing I felt there is in habits of exalted imagination. My sorrow was controlled, and my uneasiness of mind – not quieted and relieved altogether – seemed at once to receive the gift of an anchor of security.

WILLIAM WORDSWORTH,
Letter to Sir George Beaumont
8th April 1808.

NIGHT WALKS

Some years ago, a temporary inability to sleep, referable to a distressing impression, caused me to walk about the streets all night, for a series of several nights. The disorder might have taken a long time to conquer, if it had been faintly experimented on in bed; but, it was soon defeated by the brisk treatment of getting up directly after lying down, and going out, and coming home tired at sunrise.

In the course of those nights, I finished my education in a fair amateur experience of houselessness. My principal object being to get through the night, the pursuit of it brought me into sympathetic relations with people who have no other object every night in the year.

The month was March, and the weather damp, cloudy, and cold. The sun not rising before half-past five, the night perspective looked sufficiently long at half-past twelve: which was about my time for confronting it.

The restlessness of a great city, and the way in which it rumbles and tosses before it can get to sleep, formed one of the first entertainments offered to the contemplation of us houseless people. It lasted about two hours. We lost a great deal of companionship when the late public-houses turned their lamps out, and when the potmen thrust the last brawling drunkards into the street; but stray vehicles and stray people were left us, after that. If we were very lucky, a policeman's rattle sprang and a fray turned up; but in general, surprisingly little of this diversion was provided. Except in the Haymarket, which is the worst kept part of London, and about Kent Street in the Borough, and along a portion of the line of the Old Kent Road, the peace was seldom violently broken. But, it was always the case that London, as if in imitation of individual citizens belonging to it, had expiring fits and starts of restlessness. After all seemed quiet, if one cab rattled by, half a dozen would surely follow; and Houselessness even observed that intoxicated people appeared to be magnetically attracted towards each other: so that we knew when we saw one drunken object staggering against the shutters of a shop, that another drunken object would stagger up before five minutes were out, to fraternize or fight with it. When we made a divergence from the regular species of drunkard, the thin-armed, puff-faced, leaden-lipped gin-drinker, and encountered a rarer specimen of a more decent appearance, fifty to one but that specimen was dressed in soiled mourning. As the street experience in the night, so the street experience in the day; the common folk who come unexpectedly into a little property, come unexpectedly into a deal of liquor.

At length these flickering sparks would die away, worn out – the last veritable sparks of waking life trailed from some late pieman or hot-potato man – and London would sink to rest. And then the yearning of the houseless mind would be for any sign of company, any lighted place, any movement, anything suggestive of anyone being up – nay, even so much as awake, for the houseless eye looked out for lights in windows.

Walking the streets under the pattering rain, Houselessness would walk and walk and walk, seeing nothing but the interminable tangle of streets, save at a corner, here and there, two policemen in conversation, or the sergeant or inspector looking after his men. Now and then in the night – but rarely – Houselessness would become aware of a furtive head peering out of a doorway a fews yards before him, and coming up with the head, would find a man standing bolt upright to keep within the doorway's shadow, and evidently intent upon no particular service to society. Under a kind of fascination, and in a ghostly silence suitable to the time, Houselessness and this gentleman would eye one another from head to foot, and so, without exchange of speech, part, mutually suspicious. Drip, drip, drip, from ledge and coping, splash from pipes and water-spouts, and by and by the houseless shadow would fall upon the stones that pave the way to Waterloo Bridge; it being in the houseless mind to have a halfpenny worth of excuse for saying 'Good night' to the toll-keeper, and catching a glimpse

'In those small hours . . . there was no movement in the streets.'

of his fire. A good fire and a good greatcoat and a good woollen neck-shawl, were comfortable things to see in conjunction with the toll-keeper; also his brisk wakefulness was excellent company when he rattled the change of halfpence down upon that metal table of his, like a man who defied the night, with all its sorrowful thoughts, and didn't care for the coming of dawn. There was need of encouragement on the threshold of the bridge, for the bridge was dreary. The chopped-up murdered man, had not been lowered with a rope over the parapet when those nights were; he was alive, and slept then quietly enough most likely, and undisturbed by any dream of where he was to come. But the river had an awful look, the buildings on the banks were muffled in black shrouds, and the reflected lights seemed to originate deep in the water, as if the spectres of suicides were holding them to show where they went down. The wild moon and clouds were as restless as an evil conscience in a tumbled bed, and the very shadow of the immensity of London seemed to lie oppressively upon the river.

Between the bridge and the two great theatres, there was but the distance of a few hundred paces, so the theatres came next. Grim and black within, at night, those great dry Wells, and lonesome to imagine, with the rows of faces faded out, the light extinguished, and the seats all empty. One would think that nothing in them knew itself at such a time but Yorick's skull. In one of my night walks, as the church steeples were shaking the March winds and rain with strokes of Four, I passed the outer boundary of one of these great deserts, and entered it. With a dim lantern in my hand, I groped my well-known way to the stage and looked over the orchestra – which was like a great grave dug for a time of pestilence – into the void beyond. A dismal cavern of an immense aspect, with the chandelier gone dead like everything else, and nothing visible through mist and fog and space, but tiers of winding-sheets. The ground at my feet where, when last there, I had seen the peasantry of Naples dancing among the vines, reckless of the burning mountain which threatened to overwhelm them, was now in possession of a strong serpent of engine-hose, watchfully lying in wait for the serpent Fire, and ready to fly at it if it showed its forked tongue. A ghost of a watchman, carrying a faint corpse candle, haunted the distant upper gallery and flitted away. Retiring within the proscenium, and holding my light above my head towards the rolled-up curtain – green no more, but black as ebony – my sight lost itself in a gloomy vault, showing faint indications in it of a shipwreck of canvas and cordage. Methought I felt much as a diver might, at the bottom of the sea.

In those small hours when there was no movement in the streets, it afforded matter for reflection to take Newgate in the way, and, touching its rough stone, to think of the prisoners in their sleep, and then to glance in at the lodge over the spiked wicket, and see the fire and light of the watching turnkeys, on the white wall. Not an inappropriate time either, to linger by that wicked little Debtors' Door – shutting tighter than any other door one ever saw – which has been Death's Door to so many. In the days of the uttering of forged one-pound notes by people tempted up from the country, how many hundreds of wretched creatures of both sexes – many quite innocent – swung out of a pitiless and inconsistent world, with the tower of yonder Christian church of Saint Sepulchre monstrously before their eyes! Is there any haunting of the Bank Parlour, by the remorseful souls of old directors, in the nights of these later days, I wonder, or is it as quiet as this degenerate Aceldama of an Old Bailey?

To walk on to the Bank, lamenting the good old times and bemoaning the present evil period, would be an easy next step, so I would take it, and would make my houseless circuit of the Bank, and give a thought to the treasure within; likewise to the guard of soldiers passing the night there, and nodding over the fire. Next, I went to Billingsgate, in some hope of market-people, but it proving as yet too early, crossed London Bridge and got down by the waterside on the Surrey shore among the buildings of the great brewery. There was plenty going on at the brewery; and the reek, and the smell of grains, and the rattling of the plump dray horses at their mangers, were capital company. Quite refreshed by having mingled with this good society, I made a new start with a new heart, setting the old King's Bench prison before me for my next object, and resolving, when I should come to the wall, to think of poor Horace Kinch, and the Dry Rot in men.

A very curious disease the Dry Rot in men, and difficult to detect the beginning of. It had carried Horace Kinch inside the wall of the old King's Bench prison, and it had carried him out with his feet foremost. He was a likely man to look at, in the prime of life, well to do, as clever as he needed to be, and popular among many friends. He was suitably married, and had healthy and pretty children. But, like some fair-looking houses or fair-looking ships, he took the Dry Rot. The first strong external revelation of the Dry Rot in men, is a tendency to lurk and lounge; to be at street-corners without intelligible reason; to be going anywhere when met; to be about many places rather than at any; to do nothing tangible, but to have an intention of performing a variety of intangible duties to-morrow or the day after. When this manifestation of the disease is observed, the observer will usually connect it with a vague impression once formed or received, that the patient was living a little too hard. He will scarcely have had leisure to turn it over in his mind and form the terrible suspicion 'Dry Rot,' when he will notice a change for the worse in the patient's appearance: a certain slovenliness and deterioration, which is not poverty, nor dirt, nor intoxication, nor ill-health, but simply Dry Rot. To this, succeeds a smell as of strong waters, in the morning; to that, a looseness respecting money; to that, a stronger smell as of strong waters, at all times; to that, a looseness respecting everything; to that, a trembling of the limbs, somnolency, misery, and crumbling to pieces. As it is in wood, so it is in men. Dry Rot advances at a compound usury quite incalculable. A plank is found infected with it, and the whole structure is devoted. Thus it had been with the unhappy Horace Kinch, lately buried by a small subscription. Those who knew him had not nigh done saying, 'So well off, so comfortably established, with such hope before him – and yet, it is feared, with a slight touch of Dry Rot!' when lo! the man was all Dry Rot and dust.

From the dead wall associated on those houseless nights with this too common story, I chose next to wander by Bethlehem Hospital; partly, because it lay on my road round to Westminster; partly, because I had a night fancy in my head which could be best pursued within sight of its walls and dome. And the fancy was this: Are not the sane and the insane equal at night as the sane lie a-dreaming? Are not all of us outside this hospital who dream, more or less in the condition of those inside it, every night of our lives? Are we not nightly persuaded, as they daily are, that we associate preposterously with kings and queens, emperors and empresses, and nota-bilities of all sorts? Do we not nightly jumble events and personages and times and places, as these do daily? Are we not sometimes troubled by our own sleeping inconsistencies, and do we not vexedly try to account for them or excuse them, just as these do sometimes in respect of their waking delusions? Said an afflicted man to me, when I was last in a hospital like this, 'Sir, I can frequently fly.' I was half ashamed to reflect and so could I – by night. Said a woman to me on the same occasion, 'Queen Victoria frequently comes to dine with me, and Her Majesty and I dine off peaches and maccaroni in our night-gowns, and His Royal Highness the Prince Consort does us the honour to make a third on horseback in a Field-Marshal's uniform.' Could I refrain from reddening with consciousness when I remembered the amazing royal parties I myself had given (at night), the unaccountable viands I had put on table, and my extraordinary manner of conducting myself on those distinguished occasions? I wonder that the great master who knew everything, when he called Sleep the death of each day's life, did not call Dreams the insanity of each day's sanity.

By this time I had left the Hospital behind me, and was again setting towards the river; and in a short breathing space I was on Westminster Bridge, regaling my houseless eyes with the external walls of the British Parliament – the perfection of a stupendous institution, I know, and the admiration of all surrounding nations and succeeding ages, I do not doubt, but perhaps a little the better now and then for being pricked up to its work. Turning off into Old Palace Yard, the Courts of Law kept me company for a quarter of an hour; hinting in low whispers what numbers of people they were keeping awake, and how intensely wretched and horrible they were rendering the small hours to unfortunate suitors. Westminster Abbey was fine gloomy society for another quarter of an hour; suggesting a wonderful procession of its dead among the dark arches and pillars, each century more amazed by the century following it than by all the centuries going before. And indeed in those houseless night walks – which even included cemeteries where watchmen went round among the graves at stated times, and moved the tell-tale handle of an index which

The Imperial War Museum – formerly the notorious mental asylum 'Bedlam' Hospital

recorded that they had touched it at such an hour – it was a solemn consideration what enormous hosts of dead belong to one old great city, and how, if they were raised while the living slept, there would not be the space of a pin's point in all the streets and ways for the living to come out into. Not only that, but the vast armies of dead would overflow the hills and valleys beyond the city, and would stretch away all round it, God knows how far.

When a church clock strikes, on houseless ears in the dead of the might, it may be at first mistaken for company and hailed as such. But, as the spreading circles of vibration, which you may perceive at such a time with great clearness, go opening out, for ever and ever afterwards widening perhaps (as the philosopher has suggested) in eternal space, the mistake is rectified and the sense of loneliness is profounder. Once – it was after leaving the Abbey and turning my face north – I came to the great steps of St. Martin's Church as the clock was striking Three. Suddenly, a thing that in a moment more I should have trodden upon without seeing, rose up at my feet with a cry of loneliness and houselessness, struck out of it by the bell, the like of which I never heard. We then stood face to face looking at one another, frightened by one another. The creature was like a beetle-browed, hare-lipped youth of twenty, and it had a loose bundle of rags on, which it held together with one of its hands. It shivered from head to foot, and its teeth chattered, and as it stared at me – persecutor, devil, ghost, whatever it thought me – it made with its whining mouth as if it were snapping at me, like a worried dog. Intending to give the ugly object money, I put out my hand to stay it – for it recoiled as it whined and snapped – and laid my hand upon its shoulder. Instantly, it twisted out of its garment, like the young man in the New Testament, and left me standing alone with its rags in my hands.

Covent Garden Market, when it was market morning, was wonderful company. The great wagons of cabbages, with growers' men and boys lying asleep under them, and with sharp dogs from market-garden neighbourhoods looking after the whole, were as good as a party. But one of the worst

night sights I know in London, is to be found in the children who prowl about this place; who sleep in the baskets, fight for the offal, dart at any object they think they can lay their thieving hands on, dive under the carts and barrows, dodge the constables, and are perpetually making a blunt pattering on the pavement of the Piazza with the rain of their naked feet. A painful and unnatural result comes of the comparison one is forced to institute between the growth of corruption as displayed in the so much improved and cared for fruits of the earth, and the growth of corruption as displayed in these all uncared for (except inasmuch as ever-hunted) savages.

There was early coffee to be got about Covent Garden Market, and that was more company – warm company, too, which was better. Toast of a very substantial quality was likewise procurable: though the towzled-headed man who made it, in an inner chamber within the coffee-room, hadn't got his coat on yet, and was so heavy with sleep that in every interval of toast and coffee he went off anew behind the partition into complicated cross-roads of choke and snore, and lost his way directly. Into one of these establishments (among the earliest) near Bow Street, there came one morning as I sat over my houseless cup, pondering where to go next, a man in a high and long snuff-coloured coat, and shoes, and, to the best of my belief, nothing else but a hat, who took out of his hat a large cold meat pudding; a meat pudding so large that it was a very tight fit, and brought the lining of the hat out with it. This mysterious man was known by his pudding, for on his entering, the man of sleep brought him a pint of hot tea, a small loaf, and a large knife and fork and plate. Left to himself in his box, he stood the pudding on the bare table, and, instead of cutting it, stabbed it, over-hand, with the knife, like a mortal enemy; then took the knife out, wiped it on his sleeve, tore the pudding asunder with his fingers, and ate it all up. The remembrance of this man with the pudding remains with me as the remembrance of the most spectral person my houselessness encountered. Twice only was I in that establishment, and twice I saw him stalk in (as I should say, just out of bed, and presently going back to bed), take out his pudding, stab his pudding, wipe the dagger, and eat his pudding all up. He was a man whose figure promised cadaverousness, but who had an excessively red face, though shaped like a horse's. On the second occasion of my seeing him, he said huskily to the man of sleep, 'Am I red to-night?' 'You are,' he uncompromisingly answered. 'My mother,' said the spectre, 'was a red-faced woman that liked drink, and I looked at her hard when she laid in her coffin, and I took the complexion.' Somehow, the pudding seemed an unwholesome pudding after that, and I put myself in its way no more.

When there was no market, or when I wanted variety, a railway terminus with the morning mails coming in, was remunerative company. But like most of the company to be had in this world, it lasted only a very short time. The station lamps would burst out ablaze, the porters would emerge from places of concealment, the cabs and trucks would rattle to their places (the post-office carts were already in theirs), and, finally, the bell would strike up, and the train would come banging in. But there were few passengers and little luggage, and everything scuttled away with the greatest expedition. The locomotive post-offices, with their great nets – as if they had been dragging the country for bodies – would fly open as to their doors, and would disgorge a smell of lamp, an exhausted clerk, a guard in a red coat, and their bags of letters; the engine would blow and heave and perspire, like an engine wiping its forehead and saying what a run it had had; and

within ten minutes the lamps were out, and I was houseless and alone again.

But now, there were driven cattle on the high road near, wanting (as cattle always do) to turn into the midst of stone walls, and squeeze themselves through six inches' width of iron railing, and getting their heads down (also as cattle always do) for tossing-purchase at quite imaginary dogs, and giving themselves and every devoted creature associated with them a most extraordinary amount of unnecessary trouble. Now, too, the conscious, and straggling work-people were already in the streets, and, as waking life had become extinguished with the last pieman's sparks, so it began to be rekindled with the fires of the first street-corner breakfast-sellers. And so by faster and faster degrees, until the last degrees were very fast, the day came, and I was tired and could sleep. And it is not, as I used to think, going home at such times, the least wonderful thing in London, that in the real desert region of the night, the houseless wanderer is alone there. I knew well enough where to find Vice and Misfortune of all kinds, if I had chosen; but they were put out of sight, and my houselessness had many miles upon miles of streets in which it could, and did, have its own solitary way.

CHARLES DICKENS
Uncommercial Traveller.

STREET HAUNTING: A LONDON ADVENTURE

No one perhaps has ever felt passionately towards a lead pencil. But there are circumstances in which it can become supremely desirable to possess one; moments when we are set upon having an object, an excuse for walking half across London between tea and dinner. As the foxhunter hunts in order to preserve the breed of foxes, and the golfer plays in order that open spaces may be preserved from the builders, so

when the desire comes upon us to go street rambling the pencil does for a pretext, and getting up we say: 'Really I must buy a pencil,' as if under cover of this excuse we could indulge safely in the greatest pleasure of town life in winter – rambling the streets of London.

The hour should be the evening and the season winter, for in winter the champagne brightness of the air and the sociability of the streets are grateful. We are not then taunted as in the summer by the longing for shade and solitude and sweet airs from the hayfields. The evening hour, too, gives us the irresponsibility which darkness and lamplight bestow. We are no longer quite ourselves. As we step out of the house on a fine evening between four and six, we shed the self our friends know us by and become part of that vast republican army of anonymous trampers, whose society is so agreeable after the solitude of one's own room. For there we sit surrounded by objects which perpetually express the oddity of our own temperaments and enforce the memories of our own experience. That bowl on the mantelpiece, for instance, was bought at Mantua on a windy day. We were leaving the shop when the sinister old woman plucked at our skirts and said she would find herself starving one of these days, but, 'Take it' she cried, and thrust the blue and white china bowl into our hands as if she never wanted to be reminded of her quixotic generosity. So, guiltily, but suspecting nevertheless how badly we had been fleeced, we carried it back to the little hotel where, in the middle of the night, the innkeeper quarrelled so violently with his wife that we all leant out into the courtyard to look, and saw the vines laced about among the pillars and the stars white in the sky. The moment was stabilized, stamped like a coin indelibly among a million that slipped by imperceptibly. There, too, was the melancholy Englishman, who rose among the coffee cups and the little iron tables and revealed the secrets of his soul – rise up in a cloud from the china bowl on the mantelpiece. And there, as our eyes fall to the floor, is that brown stain on the carpet. Mr. Lloyd George made that. 'The man's a devil!' said Mr. Cummings, putting the kettle down with which he was about to fill the teapot so that it burnt a brown ring on the carpet.

But when the door shuts on us, all that vanishes. The shell-like covering which our souls have excreted to house themselves, to make for themselves a shape distinct from others, is broken, and there is left of all these wrinkles and roughnesses a central oyster of perceptiveness, an enormous eye. How beautiful a street is in winter! It is at once revealed and obscured. Here vaguely one can trace symmetrical straight avenues of doors and windows; here under the lamps are floating islands of pale light through which pass quickly bright men and women, who, for all their poverty and shabbiness, wear a certain look of unreality, an air of triumph, as if they had given life the slip, so that life, deceived of her prey, blunders on without them. But, after all, we are only gliding smoothly on the surface. The eye is not a miner, not a diver, not a seeker after buried treasure. It floats us smoothly down a stream; resting, pausing, the brain sleeps perhaps as it looks.

How beautiful a London street is then, with its islands of light, and its long groves of darkness, and on one side of it perhaps some tree-sprinkled, grass-grown space where night is folding herself to sleep naturally and, as one passes the iron railing, one hears those little cracklings and stirrings of leaf and twig which seem to suppose the silence of fields all round them, an owl hooting, and far away the rattle of a train in the valley. But this is London, we are reminded; high among the bare trees are hung oblong frames of reddish yellow light – windows; there are points of brilliance burning steadily like low stars – lamps; this empty ground, which holds the country in it and its peace, is only a London square, set about by offices and houses where at this hour fierce lights burn over maps, over documents, over desks where clerks sit turning with wetted forefinger the files of endless correspondences; or more suffusedly the firelight wavers and the lamplight falls upon the privacy of some drawing-room, its easy chairs, its papers, its china, its inlaid table, and the figure of a woman, accurately measuring out the precise number of spoons of tea which – She looks at the door as if she heard a ring downstairs and somebody asking, is she in?

But here we must stop peremptorily. We are in danger of digging deeper than the eye approves; we are impeding our passage down the smooth stream by catching at some branch or root. At any moment, the sleeping army may stir itself and wake in us a thousand violins and trumpets in response; the army of human beings may rouse itself and assert all its oddities and sufferings and sordidities. Let us dally a little longer, be content still with surfaces only – the glossy brilliance of the motor omnibuses; the carnal splendour of the butchers' shops with their yellow flanks and purple steaks; the blue and red bunches of flowers burning so bravely through the plate glass of the florists' windows.

In what crevices and crannies, one might ask, did they lodge, this maimed company of the halt and the blind? Here, perhaps, in the top rooms of these narrow old houses between Holborn and Soho, where people have such queer names, and pursue so many curious trades, are gold beaters, accordion pleaters, cover buttons, or support life, with even greater fantasticality, upon a traffic in cups without saucers, china umbrella handles, and highly-coloured pictures of martyred saints. There they lodge, and it seems as if the lady in the sealskin jacket must find life tolerable, passing the time of day with the accordion pleater, or the man who covers buttons; life which is so fantastic cannot be altogether tragic. They do not grudge us, we are musing, our prosperity; when, suddenly, turning the corner, we come upon a bearded Jew, wild, hunger-bitten, glaring out of his misery; or pass the humped body of an old woman flung abandoned on the step of a public building with a cloak over her like the hasty covering thrown over a dead horse or donkey. At such sights the nerves of the spine seem to stand erect; a sudden flare is brandished in our eyes; a question is asked which is never answered. Often enough these derelicts choose to lie not a stone's throw from theatres, within hearing of barrel organs, almost, as night draws on, within touch of the sequined cloaks and bright legs of diners and dancers. They lie close to those shop windows where commerce offers to a world of old women laid on doorsteps, of blind men, of hobbling dwarfs, sofas which are supported by the gilt necks of proud swans; tables inlaid with baskets of many coloured fruit; sideboards paved with green marble the better to support the weight of boars' heads; and carpets so softened with age that their carnations have almost vanished in a pale green sea.

Passing, glimpsing, everything seems accidentally but miraculously sprinkled with beauty, as if the tide of trade which deposits its burden so punctually and prosaically upon the shores of Oxford Street had this night cast up nothing but treasure. With no thought of buying, the eye is sportive and generous; it creates; it adorns; it enhances. Standing out in the street, one may build up all the chambers of an imaginary house and furnish them at one's will with sofa, table, carpet. That rug will do for the hall. That alabaster bowl shall stand on a carved table in the window. Our merrymaking shall be reflected in that thick round mirror. But, having built and furnished the house, one is happily under no obligation to possess it; one can dismantle it in the twinkling of an eye, and build and furnish another house with other chairs and other glasses. Or let us indulge ourselves at the antique jewellers, among the trays of rings and the hanging necklaces. Let us choose those pearls, for example, and then imagine how, if we put them on, life would be changed. It becomes instantly between two and three in the morning; the lamps are burning very white in the deserted streets of Mayfair. Only motor-cars are abroad at this hour, and one has a sense of emptiness, of airiness, of secluded gaiety. Wearing pearls, wearing silk, one steps out on to a balcony which overlooks the gardens of sleeping Mayfair. There are a few lights in the bedrooms of great peers returned from Court, of silk-stockinged footmen, of dowagers who have pressed the hands of statesmen. A cat creeps along the garden wall. Love-making is going on sibilantly, seductively in the darker places of the room behind thick green curtains. Strolling sedately as if he were promenading a terrace beneath which the shires and counties of England lie sun-bathed, the aged Prime Minister recounts to Lady So-and-So with the curls and the emeralds the true history of some great crisis in the affairs of the land. We seem to be riding on the top of the highest mast of the tallest ship; and yet at the same time we know that nothing of this sort matters; love is not proved thus, nor great achievements completed thus; so that we sport with the moment and preen our feathers in it lightly, as we stand on the balcony watching the moonlit cat creep along Princess Mary's garden wall.

But what could be more absurd? It is, in fact, on the stroke

'. . . The whole breadth of the River Thames — wide, mournful, peaceful.'

of six; it is a winter's evening; we are walking to the Strand to buy a pencil. How, then, are we also on a balcony, wearing pearls in June? What could be more absurd? Yet it is nature's folly, not ours. When she set about her chief masterpiece, the making of man, she should have thought of one thing only. Instead, turning her head, looking over her shoulder, into each one of us she let creep instincts and desires which are utterly at variance with his main being, so that we are streaked, variegated, all of a mixture; the colours have run. Is the true self this which stands on the pavement in January, or that which bends over the balcony in June? Am I here, or am I there? Or is the true self neither this nor that, neither here nor there, but something so varied and wandering that it is only when we give the rein to its wishes and let it take its way unimpeded that we are indeed ourselves? Circumstances compel unity; for convenience sake a man must be a whole. The good citizen when he opens his door in the evening must be banker, golfer, husband, father; not a nomad wandering the desert, a mystic staring at the sky, a debauchee in the slums of San Francisco, a soldier heading a revolution, a pariah howling with scepticism and solitude. When he opens his door, he must run his fingers through his hair and put his umbrella in the stand like the rest.

But here, none to soon, are the second-hand bookshops. Here we find anchorage in these thwarting currents of being; here we balance ourselves after the splendours and miseries of the streets. The very sight of the bookseller's wife with her foot on the fender, sitting beside a good coal fire, screened from the door, is sobering and cheerful. She is never reading, or only the newspaper; her talk, when it leaves bookselling, which it does so gladly, is about hats; she likes a hat to be practical, she says, as well as pretty. O no, they don't live at the shop; they live in Brixton; she must have a bit of green to look at. In summer a jar of flowers grown in her own garden is stood on the top of some dusty pile to enliven the shop. Books are everywhere; and always the same sense of adventure fills us. Second-hand books are wild books, homeless books; they have come together in vast flocks of variegated feather, and have a charm which the domesticated volumes of the library lack. Besides, in this random miscellaneous company we may rub against some complete stranger who will, with luck, turn into the best friend we have in the world. There is always a hope, as we reach down some greyish-white book from an upper shelf, directed by its air of shabbiness and desertion, of meeting here with a man who set out on horseback over a hundred years ago to explore the woollen market in the Midlands and Wales; an unknown traveller, who stayed at inns, drank his pint, noted pretty girls and serious customs, wrote it down stiffly, laboriously for sheer love of it (the book was published at his own expense); was infinitely prosy, busy, and mater-of-fact, and so let flow in without his knowing it the very scent of hollyhocks and the hay together with such a portrait of himself as gives him forever a seat in the warm corner of the mind's inglenook. One may buy him for eighteen pence now. He is marked three and sixpence, but the bookseller's wife, seeing how shabby the covers are and how long the book has stood there since it was bought at some sale of a gentleman's library in Suffolk, will let it go at that.

Thus, glancing round the bookshop, we make other such sudden capricious friendships with the unknown and the vanished whose only record is, for example, this little book of poems, so fairly printed, so finely engraved, too, with a portrait of the author. For he was a poet and drowned untimely, and his verse, mild as it is and formal and sententious, sends forth still a frail fluty sound like that of a piano organ played in some back street resignedly by an old Italian organ-grinder in a corduroy jacket. There are travellers, too, row upon row of them, still testifying, indomitable spinsters that they were, to the discomforts that they endured and the sunsets they admired in Greece when Queen Victoria was a girl. A tour in Cornwall with a visit to the tin mines was thought worthy of voluminous record. People went slowly up the Rhine and did portraits of each other in Indian ink, sitting reading on deck beside a coil of rope; they measured the pyramids; were lost to civilization for years; converted negroes in pestilential swamps. This packing up and going off, exploring deserts and catching fevers, settling in India for a lifetime, penetrating even to China and then returning to lead a parochial life at Edmonton, tumbles and tosses upon the dusty floor like an uneasy sea, so restless the English are, with the waves at their very door. The waters of travel and adventure seem to break upon little islands of serious effort and lifelong industry stood in jagged column upon the floor. In these piles of puce-bound volumes with gilt monograms on the back, thoughtful clergymen expound the gospels; scholars are to be heard with their hammers and their chisels chipping clear the ancient texts of Euripides and Aeschylus. Thinking, annotating, expounding goes on at a prodigious rate all around us and over everything, like a punctual, everlasting tide, washes the ancient sea of fiction. Innumerable volumes tell how Arthur loved Laura and they were separated and they were unhappy and then they met and they were happy ever after, as was the way when Victoria ruled these islands.

The number of books in the world is infinite, and one is forced to glimpse and nod and move on after a moment of talk, a flash of understanding, as, in the street outside, one catches a word in passing and from a chance phrase fabricates a lifetime. It is about a woman called Kate that they are talking, how 'I said to her quite straight last night . . . if you don't think I'm worth a penny stamp, I said . . .' But who Kate is, and to what crisis in their friendship that penny stamp refers, we shall never know; for Kate sinks under the warmth of their volubility; and here, at the street corner another page of the volume of life is laid open by the sight of two men consulting under the lamp-post. They are spelling out the latest wire from Newmarket in the stop press news. Do you think, then, that fortune will ever convert their rags into fur and broadcloth, sling them with watch-chains, and plant diamond pins where there is now a ragged open shirt? But the main stream of walkers at this hour sweeps too fast to let us ask such questions. They are wrapt, in this short passage from work to home, in some narcotic dream, now that they are free from the desk, and have the fresh air on their cheeks. They put on those bright clothes which they must hang up and lock the key upon all the rest of the day, and are great cricketers, famous actresses, soldiers who have saved their country at the hour of need. Dreaming, gesticulating, often muttering a few words aloud, they sweep over the Strand and across Waterloo Bridge whence they will be slung in long rattling trains, to some prim little villa in Barnes or Surbiton where the sight of the clock in the hall and the smell of the supper in the basement puncture the dream.

But we are come to the Strand now, and as we hesitate on the curb, a little rod about the length of one's finger begins to lay its bar across the velocity and abundance of life. 'Really I must – really I must' – that is it. Without investigating the demand, the mind cringes to the accustomed tyrant. One must, one always must, do something or other; it is not allowed one simply to enjoy one-self. Was it not for this reason that, some time ago, we fabricated the excuse, and invented the necessity of buying something? But what was it? Ah, we remember, it was a pencil. Let us go then and buy this pencil. But just as we are turning to obey the command, another self disputes the right of the tyrant to insist. The usual conflict comes about. Spread out behind the rod of duty we see the whole breadth of the river Thames – wide, mournful, peaceful. And we see it through the eyes of somebody who is leaning over the Embankment on a summer evening, without a care in the world. Let us put off buying the pencil; let us go in search of this person – and soon it becomes apparent that this person is ourselves. For if we could stand there where we stood six months ago, should we not be again as we were then – calm, aloof, content? Let us try then. But the river is rougher and greyer than we remembered. The tide is running out to sea. It brings down with it a tug and two barges, whose load of straw is tightly bound down beneath tarpaulin covers. There is, too, close by us, a couple leaning over the balustrade with the curious lack of self-consciousness lovers have, as if the importance of the affair they are engaged in claims without question the indulgence of the human race. The sights we see and the sounds we hear now have none of the quality of the past; nor have we any share in the serenity of the person who, six months ago, stood precisely where we stand now. His is the happiness of death; ours the insecurity of life. He has no future; the future is even now invading our peace. It is only when we look at the past and take from it the element of uncertainty that we can enjoy perfect peace. As it is, we must turn, we must cross the Strand again, we must find a shop where, even at this hour, they will be ready to sell us a pencil.

It is always an adventure to enter a new room; for the lives and characters of its owners have distilled their atmosphere into it, and directly we enter it we breast some new wave of emotion. Here, without a doubt, in the stationer's shop people had been quarrelling. Their anger shot through the air. They both stopped; the old woman – they were husband and wife evidently – retired to a back room; the old man whose rounded forehead and globular eyes would have looked well on the frontispiece of some Elizabethan folio, stayed to serve us. 'A pencil, a pencil,' he repeated, 'certainly, certainly.' He spoke with the distraction yet effusiveness of one whose emotions have been roused and checked in full flood. He began opening box after box and shutting them again. He said that it was very difficult to find things when they kept so many different articles. He launched into a story about some legal gentleman who had got into deep waters owing to the conduct of his wife. He had known him for years; he had been connected with the Temple for half a century, he said, as if he wished his wife in the back room to overhear him. He upset a box of rubber bands. At last, exasperated by his incompetence, he pulled the swing door open and called out roughly: 'Where d'you keep the pencils?' as if his wife had hidden them. The old lady came in. Looking at nobody, she put her hand with a fine air of righteous severity upon the right box. There were pencils. How then could he do without her? Was she not indispensable to him? In order to keep them there, standing side by side in forced neutrality, one had to be particular in one's choice of pencils; this was too soft, that too hard. They stood silently looking on. The longer they stood there, the calmer they grew; their heat was going down, their anger disappearing. Now, without a word said on either side, the quarrel was made up. The old man, who would not have disgraced Ben Jonson's title-page, reached the box back to its proper place, bowed profoundly his good-night to us, and they disappeared. She would get out her sewing; he would read his newspaper; the canary would scatter them impartially with seed. The quarrel was over.

In these minutes in which a ghost has been sought for, a quarrel composed, and a pencil bought, the streets had become completely empty. Life had withdrawn to the top floor, and lamps were lit. The pavement was dry and hard; the road was of hammered silver. Walking home through the desolation one could tell oneself the story of the dwarf, of the blind men, of the party in the Mayfair mansion, of the quarrel in the stationer's shop. Into each of these lives one could penetrate a little way, far enough to give oneself the illusion that one is not tethered to a single mind, but can put on briefly for a few minutes the bodies and minds of others. One could become a washerwoman, a publican, a street singer. And what greater delight and wonder can there be than to leave the straight lines of personality and deviate into those footpaths that lead beneath the brambles and thick tree trunks into the heart of the forest where live those wild beasts, our fellow men?

That is true: to escape is the greatest of pleasures; street haunting in winter the greatest of adventures. Still as we approach our own doorstep again, it is comforting to feel the old possessions, the old prejudices, fold us round; and the self, which has been blown about at so many street corners, which has battered like a moth at the flame of so many inaccessible lanterns, sheltered and enclosed. Here again is the usual door; here the chair turned as we left it and the china bowl and the brown ring on the carpet. And here – let us examine it tenderly, let us touch it with reverence – is the only spoil we have retrieved from all the treasures of the city, a lead pencil.

VIRGINIA WOOLF,
Street Haunting:
A London Adventure, 1930.

THAMES AND THE HOME COUNTIES

The Thames at Lechlade. Shelley wrote his finest love poetry while
indulging in his passion for boating.

47

TO JANE: THE INVITATION

Best and brightest, come away!
   Fairer far than this fair Day,
Which like thee to those in sorrow
   Hopes to bid a sweet good-morrow
To the rough Year just awake
   In its cradle on the brake.
The brightest hour of unborn Spring,
   Through the Winter wandering,
Found, it seems, the halcyon Morn
   To hoar February born.
Bending from Heaven, in azure mirth,
It kissed the forehead of the Earth,
   And smiled upon the silent sea,
And bade the frozen streams be free,
   And waked to music all their fountains,
And breathed upon the frozen mountains,
   And like a prophetess of May
Strewed flowers upon the barren way,
   Making the wintry world appear
Like one on whom thou smilest, dear.
Away, away, from men and towns,
   To the wild wood and the downs –
To the silent wilderness
   Where the soul need not repress
Its music lest it should not find
   An echo in another's mind,
While the touch of Nature's art
   Harmonizes heart to heart,
I leave this notice on my door
   For each accustomed visitor:–
'I am gone into the fields
   To take what this sweet hour yields; –
Reflection, you may come to-morrow,
   Sit by the fireside with Sorrow. –
You with the unpaid bill, Despair, –

You, tiresome verse-reciter, Care, –
I will pay you in the grave, –
   Death will listen to your stave.
Expectation too, be off!
   To-day is for itself enough;
Hope, in pity mock not woe
   With smiles, nor follow where I go;
Long having lived on thy sweet food,
   At length I find one moment's good
After long pain – with all your love,
   This you never told me of.'

Radiant Sister of the Day,
   Awake! arise! and come away!
To the wild woods and the plains,
   And the pools where winter rains
Image all their roof of leaves,
   Where the pine its garland weaves
Of sapless green and ivy dun
   Round stems that never kiss the sun;
Where the lawns and pastures be,
   And the sandhills of the sea; –
Where the melting hoar-frost wets
   The daisy-star that never sets,
And wild-flowers, and violets,
   Which yet join not scent to hue,
Crown the pale year weak and new;
   When the night is left behind
In the deep east, dun and blind,
   And the blue noon is over us,
And the multitudinous
   Billows murmur at our feet,
Where the earth and ocean meet,
   And all things seem only one
In the universal sun.

P B SHELLEY

Bisham Wood – a favourite spot where Shelley would sit in the
open air and compose.

THE SOUTH-WEST WIND

Rain was universal; a thick robe of it swept from hill to hill; thunder rumbled remote, and between the muffled roars the downpour pressed on the land with a great noise of eager gobbling, much like that of the swine's trough fresh filled, as though a vast assembly of the hungered had seated themselves clamourously and fallen to on meats and drinks in a silence, save of the chaps. A rapid walker poetically and humourously minded gathers multitudes of images on his way. And rain, the heaviest you can meet, is a lively companion when the resolute pacer scorns discomfort of wet clothes and squeaking boots. South-western rain-clouds, too, are never long sullen; they enfold and will have the earth in a good strong glut of the hissing overflow; then, as a hawk with feathers on his beak of the bird in his claw lifts head, they rise and take veiled features in long climbing watery lines: at any moment they may break the veil and show soft upper cloud, show sun on it, show sky, green near the verge they spring from, of the green of grass in early dew; or, along a travelling sweep that rolls asunder overhead, heaven's laughter of purest blue among titanic white shoulders: it may mean fair smiling for a while, or be the lightest interlude; but the watery lives, and the drifting, the

chasing, the upsoaring, all in a shadowy fingering of form, and the animation of the leaves of the trees pointing them on, the bending of the tree-tops, the snapping of branches, and the hurrahings of the stubborn hedge at wrestle with the flaws, yielding but a leaf at most, and that on a fling, make a glory of contest and wildness without aid of colour to inflame the man who is at home in them from old association on road, heath and mountain. Let him be drenched, his heart will sing. And thou, trim cockney, that jeerest, consider thyself, to whom it may occur to be out in such a scene, and that with what steps of a nervous dancing master it would be thine to play the hunted rat of the elements, for the preservation of the one imagined dry spot about thee, somewhere on thy luckless person! The taking of rain and sun alike befits men of our climate, and he who would have the secret of a strengthening intoxication must count the clouds of the south-west with a lover's blood.

GEORGE MEREDITH
The Egoist, 1879.

WALK TO BE MERRY

You, who in these days of vehement bustle, business, and competition, can still find time to travel for pleasure alone – you, who have yet to become emancipated from the thraldom of railways, carriages, and saddle-horses – patronize, I exhort you, that first and oldest-established of all conveyances, your own legs! Think on your tender partings nipped in the bud by the railway bell; think of crabbed cross-roads, and broken carriage-springs; think of luggage confided to extortionate porters, of horses casting shoes and catching colds, of

cramped legs and numbed feet, of vain longings to get down for a moment here, and to delay for a pleasant half-hour there – think of all these manifold hardships of riding at your ease; and the next time you leave home, strap your luggage on your shoulders, take your stick in your hand, set forth delivered from a perfect paraphernalia of encumbrances, to go where you will, how you will – the free citizen of the whole travelling world! Thus independent, what may you not accomplish? – what pleasure is there that you cannot enjoy? Are you an

The prevailing south-west wind is an uncompromising companion for trekkers
on the desolate downs.

artist? – you can stop to sketch every point of view that strikes your eye. Are you a philanthropist? – you can go into every cottage and talk to every human being you pass. Are you a botanist, or geologist? – you may pick up leaves and chip rocks wherever you please, the live-long day. Are you a valetudinarian? – you may physic yourself by Nature's own simple prescription, walking in fresh air. Are you dilatory and irresolute? – you may dawdle to your heart's content; you may change all your plans a dozen times in a dozen hours; you may tell 'Boots' at the inn to call you at six o'clock, may fall asleep again (ecstatic sensation!) five minutes after he has knocked at the door, and may get up two hours later, to pursue your journey, with perfect impunity and satisfaction. For, to you, what is a time-table but waste-paper? – and a 'booked place' but a relic of the dark ages? You dread, perhaps, blisters on your feet – sponge your feet with cold vinegar and water, change your socks every ten miles, and show me blisters after that, if you can! You strap on your knapsack for the first time, and five minutes afterwards feel an aching pain in the muscles at the back of your neck – walk *on*, and the aching will walk *off!* How do we overcome our first painful cuticular reminiscences of first getting on horseback? – by riding again. Apply the same rule to carrying the knapsack, and be assured of the same successful result. Again I say it, therefore, – walk, and be merry; walk, and be healthy; walk, and be your own master! – walk, to enjoy, to observe, to improve, as no riders can! – walk, and you are the best peripatetic impersonation of holiday enjoyment that is to be met with on the surface of this work-a-day world!

WILKIE COLLINS,
Rambles Beyond Railways, 1850.

OXFORD

May 3, 1866. Cold. Morning raw and wet, afternoon fine. Walked then with Addis, crossing Bablock Hythe, round by Skinner's Weir through many fields into the Witney Road. Sky sleepy blue without liquidity. Fr. Cumnor Hill saw St. Philip's and the other spires through blue haze rising pale in a pink light. On further side of the Witney road hills, just fleeced with grain or other green growth, by their dips and waves foreshortened here and there and so differenced in brightness and opacity the green on them, with delicate effect. On left, brow of the near hill glistening with very bright newly turned sods and a scarf of vivid green slanting away beyond the skyline, agst. which the clouds shewed the slightest tinge of rose or purple. Copses in grey-red or grey-yellow – the tinges immediately forerunning the opening of full leaf. Meadows skirting Seven-bridge road voluptuous green. Some oaks are out in small leaf. Ashes not out, only tufted with their fringy blooms. Hedges spring richly. Elms in small leaf, with more or less opacity. White poplars most beautiful in small grey crisp spray-like leaf. Cowslips capriciously colouring meadows in creamy drifts. Bluebells, purple orchis. Over the green water of the river passing the slums of the town and under its bridges swallows shooting, blue and purple above and shewing their amber-tinged breasts reflected in the water, their flight unsteady with wagging wings and leaning first to one side then the other. Peewits flying. Towards sunset the sky partly swept, as often, with moist white cloud, tailing off across which are morsels of grey-black woolly clouds. Sun seemed to make a bright liquid hole in this, its texture had an upward northerly sweep on drift fr. the W. marked softly in grey. Dog violets. Eastward after sunset range of clouds rising in bulky heads moulded softly in tufts or bunches of snow – so it looks – and membered somewhat elaborately, rose-coloured. Notice often imperfect fairy rings.

GERARD MANLEY HOPKINS,
Journal.

'. . . crossing Bablock Hythe, round by Skinner's Weir through many fields into the Witney Road.'

'Fr. Cumnor Hill saw St. Philip's and the other spires through
blue haze rising pale in a pink light.'

THE IMPRINTS OF HISTORY ON THE ENGLISH LANDSCAPE

Standing on Whitehorse Hill on the Great Ridgeway, at a point 18 miles south-west of Oxford and over 850ft above sea level, it is easy to appreciate the imprints of history on the English landscape. On the steep north-facing scarp of the chalk downs, 150ft below, is the White Horse itself – a beautiful but enigmatic creation some 360ft in length, which may be as old as the Neolithic or as recent as King Alfred; and to your left is the large but relatively shallow hill fort of Uffington Castle, generally thought to be of Iron Age origin, but possibly of a much earlier date. But the feature in this landscape that is probably far older than any other is the Ridgeway itself. This wide rutted track strides confidently along the main ridge of the downs and extends as far as the eye can see to east and west. It would have been an ancient monument in the time of the Romans, having been in use since the sub-Arctic climate of the last Ice Age began to ameliorate over 10,000 years ago.

If the weather is typically clear and windy, you will see, beyond the Ridgeway to the north and south, landscapes of great contrast. To the south are the downs, with their wide expansive ridges and their deep streamless valleys. Along many of the ridges you will be able to pick out the courses of other tracks similar to, if rather less distinguished-looking than, the Ridgeway itself. Today many of these tracks are green lanes or bridleways, used partly as means of access to the large farm buildings standing alone on the downs, but also, like the Ridgeway, as important recreation routes for the country-lovers of the twentieth century. These tracks, if followed more carefully on the map, are seen to connect not only the farm buildings and the settlements in the valleys, but also with the tumuli, the hill forts and the Roman villas, which are scattered in seemingly random fashion about the hills and valleys. This connection between the tracks and the ancient features testifies to the antiquity of so many rights of way in Britain – a unique heritage indeed.

The same quality of timelessness is apparent in the scenery and the paths to the north of our viewpoint on Whitehorse Hill. Looking across the flat fertile Vale of White Horse, we can pick out the clustered villages, with their small but delightful churches; the hamlets and the farmsteads surrounded by their lush green pastures and fields of billowing corn; and the narrow country lanes weaving their way from one settlement to the next.

In addition, with the aid of a pair of binoculars and a good map, you may be able to pick out the routes of some other rights of way which, although often no less ancient than the tracks on the downs to the south, are entirely different in nature. These are the paths that the villagers and farmers of medieval times used on their way to work in the fields, on their way to church, or just to visit friends and neighbours. Some of these paths may have been lost when the open fields were enclosed in later centuries; others may have come into being as trade between the different regions of Britain increased, and there were large-scale movements of cattle, sheep and goods along the drove roads and tracks that today stand silent and overgrown.

The mists of time obscure the origin of most of today's paths and tracks. Nevertheless it is clear that a great many of them, like the Ridgeway, are very old indeed. As the ice sheets retreated, and as the Stone Age hunting tribes of Europe moved northwards across Britain, they would have followed the paths – or at least the terrain – of least resistance. The clay vales of the Thames Basin and the Weald carried dense oak forest until well into the Middle Ages, but the chalk downlands carried, at most, only a light and easily penetrated beech woodland. The long unbroken chalk ridges also favoured fast migration, and it is not surprising that it is on the North and South Downs, and on the chalk hills of Berkshire, Dorset, Lincolnshire and Yorkshire, that some of the oldest and most clearly defined rights of way are to be found.

The ancient Ridgeway track, stretching as far as the eye can see east and west along the main ridge of the chalk downs, has been in use for over 10,000 years.

'To the south are the downs, with their wide expansive ridges and their
deep streamless valleys.'

The ridges offered the safest and the quickest routes, but the lack of water was (and to today's long-distance walker still is) a problem, so that other routes were established lower down the scarp face on the spring line. Thus the ancient Incknield Way, which can be traced in one form or another from the Thames near Goring right along the foot of the chalk scarp into Norfolk, came into being as an important prehistoric route. The Pilgrim's Way to Canterbury along the foot of the North Downs scarp offers another example, although some would dispute that such a track was ever used by medieval pilgrims travelling to the shrine of Thomas à Becket

DAVID SHARP

THE DOWNS AND THE SOUTH COAST

Seven Sisters, the chalk cliffs which border the South Downs, greet voyagers sailing up the English Channel.

THE DOWNS

O bold majestic downs, smooth, fair and lonely;
O still solitude, only matched in the skies;
   Perilous in steep places,
   Soft in the level races,
Where sweeping in phantom silence the cloudland flies;
With lovely undulation of fall and rise;
   Entrenched with thickets thorned,
By delicate miniature dainty flowers adorned!

I climb your crown, and lo! a sight surprising
Of sea in front uprising, steep and wide:
   And scattered ships ascending
   To heaven, lost in the blending
Of distant blues, where water and sky divide,
Urging their engines against wind and tide,
   And all so small and slow,
They seem to be wearily pointing the way they would go.

The accumulated murmur of soft plashing,
Of waves on rocks dashing and searching the sands,
   Takes my ear, in the veering
   Baffled wind, as rearing
Upright at the cliff, to the gullies and rifts he stands;
And his conquering surges scour out over the lands;
   While again at the foot of the downs
He masses his strength to recover the topmost crowns.

ROBERT BRIDGES

'With lovely undulation of fall and rise;
Entrenched with thickets thorned . . .'

FOLLOWING A RIVER

The stream invites us to follow: the impulse is so common that it might be set down as an instinct; and certainly there is no more fascinating pastime than to keep company with a river from its source to the sea. Unfortunately this is not easy in a country where running waters have been enclosed, which should be as free as the rain and sunshine to all, and were once free, when England was England still, before landowners annexed them, even as they annexed or stole the commons and shut up the footpaths and made it an offence for a man to go aside from the road to feel God's grass under his feet. Well, they have also got the road now, and cover and blind and choke us with its dust and insolently hoot-hoot at us. Out of the way, miserable crawlers, if you don't want to be smashed! They have got the roads and have a Parliament of motorists to maintain them in possession, but it yet remains to be seen whether or not they will be able to keep them.

Sometimes the way is cut off by huge thorny hedges and fences of barbed wire – man's devilish improvement on the bramble – brought down to the water's edge. The river-follower must force his way through these obstacles, in most cases greatly to the detriment of his clothes and temper; or, should they prove impassable, he must undress and go into the water. Worst of all is the thought that he is a trespasser. The pheasants crow loudly lest he should forget it. Occasionally too, in these private places he encounters men in velveteens with guns under their arms, and other men in tweeds and knickerbockers, with or without guns, and they all stare at him with amazement in their eyes, like disturbed cattle in a pasture; and sometimes they challenge him. But I must say that, although I have been sharply spoken to on several occasions, always, after a few words, I have been permitted to keep on my way. And on that way I intend to keep until I have no more strength to climb over fences and force my way through hedges, but like a blind and worn-out badger must take to my earth and die.

W H HUDSON,
Afoot in England, 1909.

STONEHENGE

Friday, 27 August 1875.
Today I paid my first visit to Stonehenge. We had breakfast before Church and immediately after service Morris and I started to walk to Stonehenge, eleven miles. Passing through the beautiful Cathedral Close and the city of Salisbury we took the Devizes road and after we had walked along that road for some six miles we saw in the dim distance the mysterious Stones standing upon the Plain. The sun was hot, but a sweet soft air moved over the Plain 'wafting' the scent of the purple heather tufts and the beds of thyme and making the delicate blue harebells tremble on their fragile stems. A beautiful little wheatear flitted before us from one stone heap to another along the side of the wheel track as we struck across the firm elastic turf. Around us the Plain heaved mournfully with great and solemn barrows, the 'grassy barrows of the happier dead'.

Soon after we left the Druid's Head and struck across the turf eastward we came in sight of the grey cluster of gigantic Stones. They stood in the midst of a green plain, and the first impression they left on my mind was that of a group of people standing about and talking together. It seemed to me as if they were ancient giants who suddenly became silent and stiffened

'They stood in the midst of a green plain . . . a group of people standing
about and talking together.'

Chanctonbury Ring is one of the largest and most impressive Iron Age hill-forts in Britain. According to legend, anyone who manages to count the trees will raise the ghosts of Julius Caesar and his legionaries.

into stone directly anyone approached, but who might at any moment become alive again, and at certain seasons, as at midnight and on Old Christmas and Midsummer's Eve, might form a true 'Chorea Gigantum' and circle on the Plain in a solemn and stately dance. It is a solemn awful place. As I entered the charmed circle of the sombre Stones I instinctively uncovered my head. It was like entering a great Cathedral Church.

FRANCIS KILVERT,
Diary.

CHANCLEBURY RING

Say what you will, there is not in the world
  A nobler sight than from this upper down.
No rugged landscape here, no beauty hurled
  From its Creator's hand as with a frown;
But a green plain on which green hills look down
  Trim as a garden plot. No other hue
Can hence be seen, save here and there the brown
  Of a square fallow, and the horizon's blue.
Dear checker-work of woods, the Sussex weald.

If a name is thine! How often I have fled
  To thy deep hedgerows and embraced each field,
Each lag, each pasture – fields which gave me birth
  And saw my youth, and which must hold me dead.

WILFRED SCAWEN BLUNT

Blunt always insisted that his spelling of Chanclebury was correct. The more usual one is Chanctonbury. It is a well-known beauty spot on the South Downs Way.

THE HILL PANTHEIST

It is injurious to the mind as well as to the body to be always in one place and always surrounded by the same circumstances. A species of thick clothing slowly grows about the mind, the pores are choked, little habits become a part of existence, and by degrees the mind is inclosed in a husk. When this began to form I felt eager to escape from it, to throw it off like heavy clothing, to drink deeply once more at the fresh fountains of life. An inspiration – a long deep breath of the pure air of thought – could alone give health to the heart.

There was a hill to which I used to resort at such periods. The labour of walking three miles to it, all the while gradually ascending, seemed to clear my blood of the heaviness accumulated at home. On a warm summer day the slow continued rise required continual effort, which carried away the sense of oppression. The familiar everyday scene was soon out of sight; I came to other trees, meadows, and fields; I began to breathe a new air and to have a fresher aspiration. I restrained my soul till I reached the sward of the hill; psyche, the soul that longed to be loose. I would write psyche always instead of soul to avoid meanings which have become attached to the word soul, but it is awkward to do so. Clumsy indeed are all words the moment the wooden stage of common-place life is left. I restrained psyche, my soul, till I reached and put my foot on the grass at the beginning of the green hill itself.

Moving up the sweet short turf, at every step my heart seemed to obtain a wider horizon of feeling; with every inhalation of rich pure air, a deeper desire. The very light of

'There the view was over a broad plain, beautiful with wheat, and
inclosed by a perfect amphitheatre of green hills.'

the sun was whiter and more brilliant here. By the time I had reached the summit I had entirely forgotten the petty circumstances and the annoyances of existence. I felt myself, myself. There was an intrenchment on the summit, and going down into the south-western side there was a spot where the outer bank had partially slipped, leaving a gap. There the view was over a broad plain, beautiful with wheat, and inclosed by a perfect amphitheatre of green hills. Through these hills there was one narrow groove, or pass, southwards, where the white clouds seemed to close in the horizon. Woods hid the scattered hamlets and farmhouses, so that I was quite alone.

I was utterly alone with the sun and the earth. Lying down on the grass, I spoke in my soul to the earth, the sun, the air, and the distant sea far beyond sight. I thought of the earth's firmness – I felt it bear me up; through the grassy couch there came an influence as if I could feel the great earth speaking to me. I thought of the wandering air – its pureness, which is its beauty; the air touched me and gave me something of itself. I spoke to the sea: though so far, in my mind I saw it, green at the rim of the earth and blue in deeper ocean; I desired to have its strength, its mystery and glory. Then I addressed the sun, desiring the soul equivalent of his light and brilliance, his endurance and unwearied race. I turned to the blue heaven over, gazing into its depth, inhaling its exquisite colour and sweetness. The rich blue of the unattainable flower of the sky drew my soul towards it, and there it rested, for pure colour is rest of heart. By these I prayed; I felt an emotion of the soul beyond all definition; prayer is a puny thing to it, and the word is a rude sign to the feeling, but I know no other.

RICHARD JEFFERIES,
The Story of My Heart, 1883.

This was a favourite walk of Jefferies in his youth from his home at Coate Farmhouse near Swindon in Wiltshire to a peak on the down. Coate Farmhouse is now the Richard Jefferies Museum.

WALKING WITH D H LAWRENCE

That Tuesday night, when I was in Shed Hall, Lawrence asked, 'What time shall you start tomorrow morning?'
'About six o'clock.'
'I think I'll come with you,' he said.

The early hour was to allow for a long day; it was twenty miles to Chichester. I arranged to walk across from Rackham and join him at the gate on the Greatham road.

We met in one of those white Sussex mists which muffle the meadows before sunrise, lying breast-high on the earth, her last dream before waking. We set out, then, in a world still asleep, the known lanes and fields were strangers, as friends sleeping become strangers. The woolly haystacks and the sheep huddled against them were not yet actual haystacks and real sheep. They were still being dreamed by the land. If a lamb had bleated, one felt the dream must break, earth stir in her bed, and shake the sleep out of her eyes. We talked in lowered voices. At that time I walked with the long lope that matched Edward's[1] negligent stride. He covered ground fast without any appearance of hurry. It was too fast for Lawrence, who soon said, 'I must teach you to walk like a tramp. When you are going to walk all day you must learn to amble and rest every mile or so.' We padded it gently to the foot of the Downs, walking rather as though we were tired at the end of the day than fresh at the start of it. The low-lying sun began to melt the mists as we climbed, unpacking the world from its lamb's-wool.

Lawrence was in his angelic, child-like mood. We found,

[1] Edward Thomas

followed, and lost the old track the Romans had made over the Downs to Chichester. We lost ourselves as well as the track, and wandered among curling valleys that led us astray. We only occasionally looked at the map. We sang scraps of songs, and every two miles lolled on the grass, where, till the dew had dried, I spread my green silk mackintosh. It was a new one, and Lawrence approved of it. We ate snacks from my knapsack, and talked when we felt like it. Our talk that day seldom touched on the things that irked him unendurably. In one of the deep bottoms, where the whitebeams looked like trees in silver blossom, he cried, 'We must be springlike!' and broke green branches and stuck them round our hats.

I have sometimes tried to recall the things we said, but what I remember of that walk was its mood. Only a few spoken sentences remain. Of Bertie he said quite simply, 'I *like* your brother Bertie.' He paused. 'But he does not speak in his real voice. Scarcely anybody lets you hear his real voice.'

The day turned out extremely hot, more June than May. In the afternoon the food I had brought was exhausted. We became thirsty, and were lost still in the hills. At teatime when we took our rest we drowsed. Thirst grew intolerable, high among the Downs, far from the smell of a pub. When we rose to go on our way, '*Shandygaff!*' cried Lawrence, and as we walked began to complain to the world, 'I want my shandy-gaff!'

We made an immortal song of it, which ran:

> My shandy! my shandy!
> I want, I want my shandy!
> Shandy, shandy, shandy,
> I want my shandygaff!

The greater our thirst, the louder we vociferated our song, consulting the map-contours for a way out of the rolling hills and valleys. The next inn was all we cared about in the world. Suddenly I halted.

'My belt!'

'Eh?'

'I've left the belt of my mackintosh where we lay down.'

He eyed me. The resting-place was at least a mile behind us.

I said, 'It's a brand-new mackintosh.'

'I like it best without a belt,' said Lawrence.

> My shandy, my shandy,
> I want my shandy gaff!

So my green mackintosh wore beltless to its end.

We climbed to a saddle of the Downs that showed us signs of man again. Ploughed fields fell to a road where cottages were, and, according to my map, an inn.

'That must be East Dean down there.'

ELEANOR FARJEON,
Edward Thomas; The Last Four Years.

ROADS

I love roads;
The goddesses that dwell
Far along invisible
Are my favourite gods.

Roads go on
While we forget, and are
Forgotten like a star
That shoots and is gone.

'We met in one of those white Sussex mists which muffle the meadows
before sunrise . . .'

'We found, followed, and lost the old track the Romans had made over
the Downs to Chichester.'

On this earth 'tis sure
We men have not made
Anything that doth fade
So soon, so long endure:

The hill road wet with rain
In the sun would not gleam
Like a winding stream
If we trod it not again.

They are lonely
While we sleep, lonelier
For lack of the traveller
Who is now a dream only.

From dawn's twilight
And all the clouds like sheep
On the mountains of sleep
They wind into the night.

The next turn may reveal
Heaven: upon the crest
The close pine clump, at rest
And black, may Hell conceal.

Often footsore, never
Yet of the road I weary,
Though long and steep and dreary,
As it winds on for ever.

Whatever the road bring
To me or take from me,
They keep me company
With their pattering.

Crowding the solitude
Of the loops over the downs,
Hushing the roar of towns
And their brief multitude.

EDWARD THOMAS

THE SOUTH WEST

TESS AND ANGEL CLARE

The country custom of unreserved comradeship out of doors during betrothal was the only custom she knew, and to her it had no strangeness; though it seemed oddly anticipative to Clare till he saw how normal a thing she, in common with all the other dairy-folk, regarded it. Thus, during this October month of wonderful afternoons they roved along the meads by creeping paths which followed the brinks of trickling tributary brooks, hopping across by little wooden bridges to the other side, and back again. They were never out of the sound of some purling weir, whose buzz accompanied their own murmuring, while the beams of the sun, almost as horizontal as the mead itself, formed a pollen of radiance over the landscape. They saw tiny blue fogs in the shadows of trees and hedges, all the time that there was bright sunshine elsewhere. The sun was so near the ground, and the sward so flat, that the shadows of Clare and Tess would stretch a quarter of a mile ahead of them, like two long fingers pointing afar to where the green alluvial reaches abutted against the sloping sides of the vale.

Men were at work here and there – for it was the season for 'taking up' the meadows, or digging the little waterways clear for the winter irrigation, and mending their banks where trodden down by the cows. The shovelfuls of loam, black as jet, brought there by the river when it was as wide as the whole valley, were an essence of soils, pounded champaigns of the past, steeped, refined, and subtilized to extraordinary richness, out of which came all the fertility of the mead, and of the cattle grazing there.

Clare hardily kept his arm round her waist in sight of these watermen, with the air of a man who was accustomed to public dalliance, though actually as shy as she who, with lips parted and eyes askance on the labourers, wore the look of a wary animal the while.

'You are not ashamed of owning me as yours before them!' she said gladly.

'O no!'

'But if it should reach the ears of your friends at Emminster that you are walking about like this with me, a milkmaid –'

'The most bewitching milkmaid ever seen.'

'They might feel it a hurt to their dignity.'

'My dear girl – a d'Urberville hurt the dignity of a Clare! It is a grand card to play – that of your belonging to such a family, and I am reserving it for a grand effect when we are married, and have the proofs of your descent from Parson Tringham. Apart from that, my future is to be totally foreign to my family – it will not affect even the surface of their lives. We shall leave this part of England – perhaps England itself – and what does it matter how people regard us here? You will like going, will you not?'

She could answer no more than a bare affirmative, so great was the emotion aroused in her at the thought of going through the world with him as his own familiar friend. Her feelings almost filled her ears like a babble of waves, and surged up to her eyes. She put her hand in his, and thus they went on, to a place where the reflected sun glared up from the river, under a bridge, with a molten-metallic glow that dazzled their eyes, though the sun itself was hidden by the bridge. They stood still, whereupon little furred and feathered heads popped up from the smooth surface of the water; but, finding that the disturbing presences had paused, and not passed by, they disappeared again. Upon this river-brink they lingered till the fog began to close round them – which was very early in the evening at this time of the year – settling on the lashes of her eyes, where it rested like crystals, and on his brows and hair.

THOMAS HARDY,
Tess of the D'Urbervilles, 1891.

THE WEARY WALKER

A plain in front of me,
    And there's the road
Upon it. Wide country,
    And, too, the road!

Past the first ridge another,
    And still the road
Creeps on. Perhaps no other
    Ridge for the road?

Ah! Past that ridge a third,
    Which still the road
Has to climb furtherward –
    The thin white road!

Sky seems to end its track;
    But no. The road
Trails down the hill at the back.
    Ever the road!

In this poem Hardy recalls trudging home from Dorchester to Higher Brockhampton in his youth.

THOMAS HARDY

'. . . they roved along the meads by creeping paths which followed the brinks of trickling tributary brooks, hopping across by little wooden bridges to the other side, and back again.'

'The thin white road' from Stinsford to Brockhampton.

THE MIDLANDS

OAK AND OLIVE

I

Though I was born a Londoner,
   And bred in Gloucestershire,
I walked in Hellas years ago
   With friends in white attire;
And I remember how my soul
   Drank wine as pure as fire.

And when I stand by Charing Cross
   I can forget to hear
The crash of all those smoking wheels,
   When those cold flutes and clear
Pipe with such fury down the street,
   My hands grow moist with fear.

And there's a hall in Bloomsbury
   No more I dare to tread,
For all the stone men shout at me
   And swear they are not dead;
And once I touched a broken girl
   I knew that marble bled.

II

But when I walk in Athens town
   That swims in dust and sun,
Perverse, I think of London then,
   Where massive work is done,
And with what sweep at Westminster
   The rayless waters run.

I ponder how from Attic seed
   There grew an English tree,
How Byron like his heroes fell,
Fighting a country free.
And Swinburne took from Shelley's lips
   This Kiss of Poetry.

And while our poets chanted Pan
   Back to his pipes and power,
Great Verrall, bending at his desk,
   And searching hour on hour
Found out old gardens, where the wise
   May pluck a Spartan flower.

III

When I go down the Gloucester lanes
   My friends are deaf and blind:
Fast as they turn their foolish eyes
   The Maenads leap behind,
And when I hear the fire-winged feet,
   They only hear the wind.

Have I not chased the fluting Pan
   Through Cranham's sober trees?
Have I not sat on Painswick Hill
   With a nymph upon my knees,
And she as rosy as the dawn,
   And naked as the breeze?

IV

But when I lie in Grecian fields,
   Smothered in asphodel,
Or climb the blue and barren hills,
   Or sing in woods that smell
With such hot spices of the South
   As mariners might sell –

V

Then my heart turns where no sun burns,
    To lands of glittering rain,
To fields beneath low-clouded skies
    New-widowed of their grain,
And Autumn leaves like blood and gold
    That strew a Gloucester lane.

Oh, well I know sweet Hellas now,
    And well I knew it then,
When I with starry lads walked out –
    But ah, for home again!
Was I not bred in Gloucestershire,
    One of the Englishmen!

J E FLECKER

NO TRESPASSERS

On a frosty morning with a little February sun, Clifford and Connie went for a walk across the park to the wood. That is, Clifford chuffed in his motor-chair, and Connie walked beside him.

The hard air was still sulphurous, but they were both used to it. Round the near horizon went the haze, opalescent with frost and smoke, and on the top lay the small blue sky; so that it was like being inside an enclosure, always inside. Life always a dream or a frenzy, inside an enclosure . . .

Clifford steered cautiously down the slope of the knoll from the hall, and Connie kept her hand on the chair. In front lay the wood, the hazel thicket nearest, the purplish density of oaks beyond. From the wood's edge rabbits bobbed and nibbled. Rooks suddenly rose in a black train, and went trailing off over the little sky.

Connie opened the wood-gate, and Clifford puffed slowly through into the broad riding that ran up an incline between the clean-whipped thickets of the hazel. The wood was a remnant of the great forest where Robin Hood hunted, and this riding was an old, old thoroughfare coming across country. But now, of course, it was only a riding through the private wood. The road from Mansfield swerved round to the north . . .

In the wood everything was motionless, the old leaves on the ground keeping the frost on their underside. A jay called harshly, many little birds fluttered. But there was no game; no pheasants. They had been killed off during the war, and the wood had been left unprotected, till now Clifford had got his game-keeper again.

Clifford loved the wood; he loved the old oak trees. He felt they were his own through generations. He wanted to protect them. He wanted this place inviolate, shut off from the world.

The chair chuffed slowly up the incline, rocking and jolting on the frozen clods. And suddenly, on the left, came a clearing where there was nothing but a ravel of dead bracken, a thin and spindly sapling leaning here and there, big sawn stumps, showing their tops and their grasping roots, lifeless. And patches of blackness where the woodmen had burned the brushwood and rubbish . . .

Clifford sat with a fixed face as the chair slowly mounted. When they came to the top of the rise he stopped; he would not risk the long and very jolty down-slope. He sat looking at the greenish sweep of the riding downwards, a clear way through the bracken and oaks. It swerved at the bottom of the hill and disappeared; but it had such a lovely easy curve, of knights riding and ladies on palfreys.

'To fields beneath low-clouded skies
New-widowed of their grain . . .'

'And Autumn leaves like blood and gold
That strew a Gloucester lane.'

'I consider this is really the heart of England,' said Clifford to Connie, as he sat there in the dim February sunshine.

'Do you?' she said, seating herself in her blue knitted dress, on a stump by the path.

'I do! this is the old England, the heart of it; and I intend to keep it intact.'

'Oh yes!' said Connie. But, as she said it she heard the eleven-o'clock hooters at Stacks Gate Colliery. Clifford was too used to the sound to notice.

'I want this wood perfect . . . untouched. I want nobody to trespass in it,' said Clifford.

D H LAWRENCE,
Lady Chatterley's Lover.

GOING OUT FOR A WALK

It is a fact that not once in all my life have I gone out for a walk. I have been taken out for walks; but that is another matter. Even while I trotted prattling by my nurse's side I regretted the good old days when I had, and wasn't, a perambulator. When I grew up it seemed to me that the one advantage of living in London was that nobody ever wanted me to come out for a walk. London's very drawbacks – its endless noise and hustle, its smoky air, the squalor ambushed everywhere in it – assured this one immunity. Whenever I was with friends in the country, I knew that at any moment, unless rain were actually falling, some man might suddenly say, 'Come out for a walk!' in that sharp imperative tone which he would not dream of using in any other connection. People seem to think there is something inherently noble and virtuous in the desire to go for a walk. Any one thus desirous feels that he has a right to impose his will on whomever he sees comfortably settled in an arm-chair, reading. It is easy to say simply 'No' to an old friend. In the case of a mere acquaintance one wants some excuse. 'I wish I could, but' – nothing ever occurs to me except 'I have some letters to write.' This formula is unsatisfactory in three ways. (1) It isn't believed. (2) It compels you to rise from your chair, go to the writing-table, and sit improvising a letter to somebody until the walkmonger (just not daring to call you liar and hypocrite) shall have lumbered out of the room. (3) It won't operate on Sunday mornings. 'There's no post out till this evening' clinches the matter; and you may as well go quietly.

Walking for walking's sake may be as highly laudable and exemplary a thing as it is held to be by those who practise it. My objection to it is that it stops the brain. Many a man has professed to me that his brain never works so well as when he is swinging along the high road or over hill and dale. This boast is not confirmed by my memory of anybody who on a Sunday morning has forced me to partake of his adventure. Experience teaches me that whatever a fellow-guest may have of power to instruct or to amuse when he is sitting on a chair, or standing on a hearth-rug, quickly leaves him when he takes one out for a walk. The ideas that came so thick and fast to him in any room, where are they now? Where that encyclopaedic knowledge which he bore so lightly? Where the kindling fancy that played like summer lightning over any topic that was started? The man's face that was so mobile is set now; gone is the light from his fine eyes. He says that A. (our host) is a thoroughly good fellow. Fifty yards further on, he adds that A. is one of the best fellows he has ever met. We tramp another furlong or so, and he says that Mrs. A. is a charming woman. Presently he adds that she is one of the most charming women he has ever known. We pass an inn. He reads vapidly aloud to me. 'The King's Arms. Licensed to sell Ales and Spirits.' I foresee that during the rest of the walk he will read aloud any inscription that occurs. We pass a 'Uxminster. 11 Miles.' We turn a sharp corner at the foot of a hill. He points at the wall, and says 'Drive Slowly.' I see far ahead, on the other side of the hedge bordering the high road, a small notice-board. He sees it too. He keeps his eye on it. And in due course 'Trespassers.' he says, 'Will be Prosecuted.' Poor man! – mentally a wreck.

Luncheon at the A.'s, however, salves him and floats him in full sail. Behold him once more the life and soul of the party. Surely he will never, after the bitter lesson of this morning, go out for another walk. An hour later, I see him striding forth, with a new companion. I watch him out of sight. I know what he is saying. He is saying that I am rather a dull man to go a walk with. He will presently add that I am one of the dullest men he ever went a walk with. Then he will devote himself to reading out the inscriptions.

I am not one of those extremists who must have a vehicle to every destination. I never go out of my way, as it were, to avoid exercise. I take it as it comes, and take it in good part. That valetudinarians are always chattering about it, and indulging in it to excess, is no reason for despising it. I am inclined to think that in moderation it is rather good for one, physically. But, pending a time when no people wish me to go and see them, and I have no wish to go and see any one, and there is nothing whatever for me to do off my own premises, I never will go out for a walk.

MAX BEERBOHM,
And Even Now, 1918.

CAMBRIDGESHIRE

But if I did not gain much from Cambridge I gained all the world from Cambridgeshire! Oh how can I express my deep, my indurated, my passionate, my unforgettable, my *eternal* debt, to that dull, flat, monotonous, tedious, unpicturesque Cambridgeshire landscape? How those roads out of Cambridge – and it seems as if all my most heavenly roads have been out of, rather than into somewhere – come back to my mind now! Those absurd little eminences known as the Gog and Magog hills: that long interminable road that leads to some pastoral churchyard that once claimed precedence of Stoke Poges as the site of the Elegy: that more beguiling, but not *very* beguiling road that led in the Ely direction, past the

place where my father's father, when a fellow of Corpus, used to go courting: those meadows towards Grantchester where there is that particular massive and wistful effect about the poplars and willows that always makes me think of Northwold: these are my masters, my fellows, my libraries, my lecture-halls; these are my Gothic shrines! And not only these in their large aspects, but every swamp-pool, every rushy brook, every weedy estuary, every turnip-field, every grey milestone, every desolate haystack became part of my spirit.

JOHN COWPER POWYS,
Autobiography.

'I want this wood perfect . . . untouched. I want nobody to trespass in it . . .'

A road out of Cambridge through 'dull, flat, monotonous, tedious,
unpicturesque Cambridgeshire landscape . . .'

The massive and wistful' poplars and willows of Grantchester meadows.

COTSWOLD WAYS

One comes across the strangest things in walks;
    Fragments of Abbey tithe-barns fixed in modern
And Dutch-sort houses where the water baulks
    Weired up, and brick kilns broken among fern,
Old troughs, great stone cisterns bishops might have
      blessed
    Ceremonially, and worthy mounting-stones;
Black timber in red brick, queerly places
    Where Hill stone was looked for – and a manor's
      bones
Spied in the frame of some wisteria'd house
    And mill-falls and sedge pools and Saxon faces
Stream-sources happened upon in unlikely places,
    And Roman-looking hills of small degree
And the surprise of dignity of poplars
    At a road end, or the white Cotswold scars,
Or sheets spread white against the hazel tree.
    Strange the large difference of up Cotswold ways;
Birdlip climbs bold and treeless to a bend,
    Portway to dim wood-lengths without end,
And Crickley goes to cliffs are the crown of days.

IVOR GURNEY

'Birdlip climbs bold and treeless to a bend,
Portway to dim wood-lengths without end . . .'

THE LAKE DISTRICT AND THE NORTH

RYDALE

March 18th (Thursday) [1802]
A very fine morning. The sun shone, but it was far colder than yesterday. I felt myself weak and William charged me not to go to Mrs. Lloyd's. I seemed indeed to myself unfit for it, but when he was gone I thought I would get the visit over if I could, so I ate a beefsteak thinking it would strengthen me; so it did, and I went off. I had a very pleasant walk – Rydale vale was full of life and motion. The wind blew briskly, and the lake was covered all over with bright silver waves, that were there each the twinkling of an eye, then others rose up and took their place as fast as they went away. The rocks glittered in the sunshine, the crows and ravens were busy, and the thrushes and little birds sang. I went through the fields, and sate ½ an hour afraid to pass a cow. The cow looked at me, and I looked at the cow, and whenever I stirred the cow gave over eating. I was not very much tired when I reached Lloyd's – I walked in the garden – Charles is all for agriculture – and Mrs. L. in her kindest way. A parcel came in from Birmingham, with Lamb's play for us, and for C.[1] They came with me as far as Rydale. As we came along Ambleside vale in the twilight it was a grave evening. There was something in the air that compelled me to serious thought – the hills were large, closed in by the sky. It was nearly dark when I parted from the Lloyds, that is night was come on, and the moon was overcast. But, as I climbed Moss,[2] the moon came out from behind a mountain mass of black clouds. O, the unutterable darkness of the sky, and the earth below the moon! There was a vivid sparkling streak of light at this end of Rydale water, but the rest was very dark, and Loughrigg Fell and Silver How were white and bright, as if they were covered with hoar frost. The moon retired again, and appeared and disappeared several times before I reached home.

DOROTHY WORDSWORTH,
Journals.

[1] Samuel Taylor Coleridge
[2] White Moss Common

ULLSWATER

APRIL
Wednesday 14th 1802. William did not rise till dinner time. I walked with Mrs C.[1] I was ill out of spirits – disheartened. Wm and I took a long walk in the Rain.
Thursday 15th. It was a threatening misty morning – but mild. We set off after dinner from Eusemere. Mrs Clarkson went a short way with us but turned back. The wind was furious and we thought we must have returned. We first rested in the large Boat-house, then under a furze Bush opposite Mr Clarkson's. Saw the plough going in the field. The wind seized our breath, the Lake was rough. There was a Boat by itself floating in the middle of the Bay below Water Millock. We rested again in the Water Millock Lane. The hawthorns are black and green, the birches here and there greenish but there is yet more of purple to be seen on the Twigs. We got over into a field to avoid some cows – people working, a few primroses by the roadside, wood-sorrel flower, the anemone, scentless violets, strawberries, and that starry yellow flower which Mrs C. calls

Rydale Vale – 'full of life and motion' when Dorothy Wordsworth
walked through on her way to Mrs Lloyds.

The path beside Rydale water where 'the rocks glittered in the sunshine . . .'

The 'large Boat-house' on the shores of Ullswater where William and Dorothy
sheltered from the wind and rain.

Ullswater – at the heart of country noted for its mountains, lakes
and valleys – a walking area beloved of the Wordsworths.

pile wort. When we were in the woods beyond Gowbarrow park we saw a few daffodils close to the water side. We fancied that the lake had floated the seeds ashore and that the little colony had so sprung up. But as we went along there were more and yet more and at last under the boughs of the trees, we saw that there was a long belt of them along the shore, about the breadth of a country turnpike road. I never saw daffodils so beautiful; they grew among the mossy stones about and about them, some rested their heads upon these stones as on a pillow for weariness and the rest tossed and reeled and danced and seemed as if they verily laughed with the wind that blew upon them over the lake, they looked so gay ever glancing ever changing. This wind blew directly over the lake to them. There was here and there a little knot and a few stragglers a few yards higher up but they were so few as not to disturb the simplicity and unity and life of that one busy highway. We rested again and again. The Bays were stormy, and we heard the waves at different distances and in the middle of the water like the sea.

DOROTHY WORDSWORTH,
Grasmere Journal.

---

[1] Mrs Coleridge

Dorothy Wordsworth was in the habit of writing up her *Journal* within three or four days of the events. William drew sustenance for his poetry from Dorothy's *Journal*. He would make her read out a passage which could revive his memory. It was two years later in 1804 that William wrote his famous poem which begins 'I wandered lonely as a cloud' recalling seeing the host of golden daffodils.

SKIDDAW

We have clambered up to the top of Skiddaw, and I have waded up the bed of Lodore. In fine, I have satisfied myself, that there is such a thing as that which tourists call *romantic*, which I very much suspected before: they make such a spluttering about it, and toss their splendid epithets around them till they give as dim a light as at four o'clock next morning the lamps do after an illumination. Mary was excessively tired, when she got about half-way up Skiddaw, but we came to a cold rill (than which nothing can be imagined more cold, running over cold stones), and with the reinforcement of a draught of cold water she surmounted it most manfully. Oh, its fine black head, and the bleak air atop of it, with a prospect of mountains all about, making you giddy; and then Scotland afar off, and the border countries so famous in song and ballad! It was a day that will stand out, like a mountain, I am sure, in my life. But I am returned (I have now been come home near three weeks – I was a month out), and you cannot conceive the degradation I felt at first, from being accustomed to wander free as air among mountains, and bathe in rivers without being controlled by any one, to come home and *work*. I felt very *little*. I had been dreaming I was a very great man.

But that is going off, and I find I shall conform in time to that state of life to which it has pleased God to call me. Besides, after all, Fleet-Street and the Strand are better places to live in for good and all than among Skiddaw. Still, I turn back to those great places where I wandered about, participating in their greatness. After all, I could not *live* in Skiddaw. I could spend a year – two, three years – among them, but I must have a prospect of seeing Fleet-Street at the end of that time, or I should mope and pine away, I know. Still, Skiddaw is a fine creature.

CHARLES LAMB
Letter to Thomas Manning
24th September 1802.

The smooth-sided, softly rounded shape of Skiddaw, 'a fine creature',
seen from across Bassenthwaite lake.

EXCURSION UP FAIRFIELD

Love's Nest [near Ambleside]
July 8th 1810

To Miss Winkley

A party was made up to go on the top of Fairfield, a high mountain a few miles from here. I made one; we were fifteen in number, besides four men who attended and carried provisions, etc. Mrs. Pedder, Miss Rhodes, Miss Barton, and myself, left home soon after five o'clock in the morning, in a cart, Mr. Pedder on a poney, and the footman on an ass. We stopped to breakfast at a Mr. Scambler's, in Ambleside, two miles from here, where the rest of the party joined us. Soon after six, we proceeded, the ladies in carts, the gentlemen on foot – Mr. Pedder and Mr. Partridge, senior, excepted. We travelled up a very steep, and a very rocky, rugged road, for five or six miles. Were you to see such a road, you would be astonished how any horse could drag a load up it, for such a length of way; it is one continued steep, without any respite for the poor animals. Fearless as I in general am, I could not divest myself of some anxiety, until we arrived at the place where we should each be obliged to trust to our own feet alone. The other ladies screamed several times, expecting to be either overturned, or precipitated backwards. No accidents, however, happened.

When arrived at the extremity of Scandale, from whence we were to *begin* to ascend, we alighted from our vehicles, and proceeded on foot. The provisions were taken out of the carts and placed upon the ass, which had been brought for the purpose. We were, altogether, as odd a group as ever were assembled. Our companion, the ass, afforded us much entertainment. Mr. Partridge, junior, by way of announcing our arrival at the foot of the mountain, blew a horn he had brought with him. He is a very conceited, pedantic, though clever young man, and appeared to fancy he blew the horn with *so much* grace! though he made it sound as like the braying of an ass as ever I heard. The ass mistook the sound as

proceeding from a fellow creature in reality, and set up such a tremendous bray that every echo in the mountains resounded. Our laughter was scarcely less loud on hearing such a comical reply; peal succeeded peal for some time. Mr. P. jun., though he could not help joining in the laugh, was not a little disconcerted at being so *egregiously* mistaken by the animal; this added still more to our mirth.

After labouring up the steep for an hour or two, over moss and rocks, we at length reached the summit. We immediately began to search for a convenient resting-place where we could sit and make our repast, and finding a very snug one where we were sheltered from the bitter cold wind, we all sat down upon the ground, and enjoyed a hearty meal of veal, ham, chicken, goosebery pies, bread, cheese, butter, hung leg of mutton, wine, porter, rum, brandy, and bitters. When our hunger was appeased, we began to stroll about and enjoy the extensive prospect. We had several prospect glasses, and the air was very clear. I was much pleased, though awed, by the trememdous rocks and precipices in various directions. I crept to the edge of several of them; but of one in particular, when I found myself seated upon its projecting point, and a direct perpendicular descent on every side but one, of many hundred yards, the sheep and the cattle beneath scarcely visible, such a degree of terror overpowered me, I durst no longer behold it. I closed my eyes, and laying flat down upon a surface just large enough to contain me, I remained a considerable time before I dared rise and make a retreat.

The mountain is shaped very like a horse shoe; we ascended at one end, and descended at the other, making a circuit of eight or ten miles at least; some say, twelve.

In descending, one or two of the party who had not provided nails in the soles of their shoes to make their footing firm, were obliged to sit down frequently, and descend by sliding; the mountain heath and moss glaze the shoes in such a manner when without nails, it is impossible to stand, much

'We travelled up a very steep, and a very rocky, rugged road, for
five or six miles.'

The rock-strewn summit of Fairfield where the party ate a 'hearty meal of veal, ham, chicken, gooseberry pies, bread, cheese, butter, hung leg of mutton, wine, porter, rum, brandy, and bitters.'

The view from the summit of Fairfield where Miss Weeton was 'much pleased, though awed, by the tremendous rocks and precipices in various directions.'

less to walk with safety where the ground is not perfectly level.

At the foot of Fairfield, we again ascended our *carriage*, and arrived in Ambleside about five o'clock, and concluded the evening at Scambler's. I have never in my life enjoyed a more agreeable excursion; such a scramble exactly suited me. To me, there is little pleasure in a straight forward walk on level ground. A fine, noble, lofty, rugged mountain, has far more charms for me than a fine, formal, artificial walk in a garden or pleasure-ground.

ELLEN WEETON
Journal of a Governess.

ASCENT OF SKIDDAW

It promised all along to be fair and we fagged and tugged nearly to the top when at half past six, there came a mist upon us and shut out the view. We did not, however, lose anything by it; we were high enough without mist to see the coast of Scotland, the Irish Sea, the hills beyond Lancaster, and nearly all the large ones of Cumberland and Westmoreland, particularly Helvellyn and Scawfell. It grew colder and colder as we ascended and we were glad, at about three parts of the way, to taste a little rum which the guide brought with him, mixed, mind ye, with mountain water. I took two glasses going and one returning. It is about six miles from where I am writing to the top; so we have walked ten miles before breakfast to-day. We went up with two others, very good sort of fellows. All felt on arising into the cold air, that same elevation which a cold bath gives one. I felt as I were going to a tournament.

JOHN KEATS,
Letter to his brother Tom
29th June 1818.

LETTER FROM KESWICK

I have taken a long solitary ramble to-day. These gigantic mountains piled on each other, these waterfalls, these million shaped clouds tinted by the varying colours of innumerable rainbows hanging between yourself and a lake as smooth and dark as a plain of polished jet, – oh! these are sights admirable to the contemplative. I have been much struck by the grandeur of its imagery. Nature here sports in the awful waywardness of her solitude; the summits of the loftiest of these immense piles of rock seem but to elevate Skiddaw and Helvellyn. Imagination is resistlessly compelled to look back upon the myriad ages whose silent change placed them here, to look back when, perhaps this retirement of peace and mountain was the pandemonium of druidical imposture, the scene of Roman pollution, the resting place of the savage denizen of these solitudes with the wolf.

P B SHELLEY,
Letter to Elizabeth Hitchener[1]
from Keswick, 1811.

---

[1] Elizabeth Hitchener was a schoolmistress in Sussex with whom Shelley formed an intellectual friendship.

The path to the summit of Skiddaw on a more pleasant day than when Keats made his ascent of this fine Lakeland peak.

'. . . these waterfalls . . . oh! these are sights
admirable to the contemplative.'

'. . . a lake as smooth and dark as a plain of polished jet . . .'

THE SANDS

Our school was not situated in the heart of the town: on entering A——— from the north-west there is a row of respectable-looking houses, on each side of the broad, white road, with narrow slips of garden-ground before them. Venetian blinds to the windows, and a flight of steps leading to each trim, brass-handled door. In one of the largest of these habitations dwelt my mother and I, with such young ladies as our friends and the public chose to commit to our charge. Consequently, we were a considerable distance from the sea, and divided from it by a labyrinth of streets and houses. But the sea was my delight; and I would often gladly pierce the town to obtain the pleasure of a walk beside it, whether with the pupils, or alone with my mother during the vacations. It was delightful to me at all times and seasons, but especially in the wild commotion of a rough sea-breeze, and in the brilliant freshness of a summer morning.

I awoke early on the third morning after my return from Ashby Park – the sun was shining through the blind, and I thought how pleasant it would be to pass through the quiet town and take a solitary ramble on the sands while half the world was in bed. I was not long in forming the resolution, nor slow to act upon it. Of course I would not disturb my mother, so I stole noiselessly downstairs, and quietly unfastened the door. I was dressed and out, when the church clock struck a quarter to six. There was a feeling of freshness and vigour in the very streets, and when I got free of the town, when my foot was on the sands and my face towards the broad, bright bay, no language can describe the effect of the deep, clear azure of the sky and ocean, the bright morning sunshine on the semi-circular barrier of craggy cliffs surmounted by green swelling hills, and on the smooth, wide sands, and the low rocks out at sea – looking, with their clothing of weeds and moss, like little grass-grown islands – and above all, on the brilliant, sparkling waves. And then, the unspeakable purity and freshness of the air! There was just enough wind to keep the whole sea in motion, to make the waves come bounding to the shore, foaming and sparkling, as if wild with glee. Nothing else was stirring – no living creature was visible besides myself. My footsteps were the first to press the firm, unbroken sands; nothing before had trampled them since last night's flowing tide had obliterated the deepest marks of yesterday, and left it fair and even, except where the subsiding water had left behind it the traces of dimpled pools and little running streams.

Refreshed, delighted, invigorated, I walked along, forgetting all my cares, feeling as if I had wings to my feet, and could go at least forty miles without fatigue, and experiencing a sense of exhilaration to which I had been an entire stranger since the days of early youth.

ANNE BRONTË,
Agnes Grey.

SOLITUDE AND COMPANIONSHIP

The glories of cloudland, the white mountains with their billowy clefts, lie along the horizon, rather than in the dome of the sky. They are frescoes on the walls, rather than on the ceiling, of heaven. Sunrise and sunset often paint upon them their pictures of an hour, unseen by us, behind some neighbouring grove or hill. Still more often do Alpine or Cumbrian mountains, from their very height and the nearness of one giant to another, hide the wealth of heaven from the

'It is the land of the far horizons, where the piled or drifted shapes of gathered vapour are for ever moving along the farthest ridge of hills . . .'

climber on the hillside, who has, however, in those lands his terrestrial compensations. In fen country the clouds are seen, but at the price of an earth of flat disillusionment. In Northumberland alone both heaven and earth are seen; we walk all day on long ridges, high enough to give far views of moor and valley, and the sense of solitude above the world below, yet so far distant from each other, and of such equal height, that we can watch the low skirting clouds as they 'post o'er land and ocean without rest'. It is the land of the far horizons, where the piled or drifted shapes of gathered vapour are for ever moving along the farthest ridge of hills, like the procession of long primaeval ages that is written in tribal mounds and Roman camps and Border towers on the breast of Northumberland.

G M TREVELYAN
The Middle Marches.

WALES AND MONMOUTH
ASCENT OF SNOWDON

In one of those excursions (may they ne'er
  Fade from remembrance!) through the Northern tracts
Of Cambria ranging with a youthful friend,
  I left Bethgelert's huts at couching-time,
And westward took my way, to see the sun
  Rise, from the top of Snowdon. To the door
Of a rude cottage at the mountain's base
  We came, and roused the shepherd who attends
The adventurous stranger's steps, a trusty guide;
  Then, cheered by short refreshment, sallied forth.
It was a close, warm, breezeless summer night,
  Wan, dull, and glaring, with a dripping fog
Low-hung and thick that covered all the sky;
  But, undiscouraged, we began to climb
The mountain-side. The mist soon girt us round,
  And, after ordinary travellers' talk
With our conductor, pensively we sank
  Each into commerce with his private thoughts:
Thus did we breast the ascent, and by myself
  Was nothing either seen or heard that checked
Those musings or diverted, save that once
  The shepherd's lurcher, who, among the crags,

Had to his joy unearthed a hedgehog, teased
  His coiled-up prey with barkings turbulent.
This small adventure, for even such it seemed
  In that wild place and at the dead of night,
Being over and forgotten, on we wound
  In silence as before. With forehead bent
Earthward, as if in opposition set
  Against an enemy, I panted up
With eager pace, and less eager thoughts.
  Thus might we wear a midnight hour away,
Ascending at loose distance each from each,
  And I, as chanced, the foremost of the band;
When at my feet the ground appeared to brighten,
  And with a step or two seemed brighter still;
Nor was time given to ask or learn the cause,
  For instantly a light upon the turf
Fell like a flash, and lo! as I looked up,
  The Moon hung naked in a firmament
Of azure without cloud, and at my feet
  Rested a silent sea of hoary mist.
A hundred hills their dusky backs upheaved
  All over this still ocean; and beyond,

ABOVE AND OPPOSITE
'I left Bethgelert's huts at couching-time,
And westward took my way, to see the sun
Rise, from the top of Snowdon.'

'When at my feet the ground appeared to brighten,
And with a step or two seemed brighter still . . .' – moonrise on Snowdon.

Far, far beyond, the solid vapours stretched,
   In headlands, tongues, and promontory shapes,
Into the main Atlantic, that appeared
   To dwindle, and give up his majesty,
Usurped upon far as the sight could reach.
   Not so the ethereal vault; encroachment none
Was there, nor loss; only the inferior stars
   Had disappeared, or shed a fainter light
In the clear presence of the full-orbed Moon,
   Who, from her sovereign elevation, gazed
Upon the billowy ocean, as it lay
   All meek and silent, save that through a rift –
Not distant from the shore whereon we stood,
   A fixed, abysmal, gloomy, breathing-place –

Mounted the roar of waters, torrents, streams
   Innumerable, roaring with one voice!
Heard over earth and sea, and, in that hour,
   For so it seemed, felt by the starry heavens.

WILLIAM WORDSWORTH

Ascent of Snowdon describes the midnight climb from Bedgelert to the summit of Snowdon to see the sunrise during Wordsworth's three-week tour of North Wales in 1791. Wordsworth was accompanied by his Cambridge friend, Robert Jones, who had been his companion on his tour of France and Switzerland the previous year. The extract was written in 1804, originally as the opening to the fifth book of *The Prelude* but subsequently transferred to the fourteenth. Many of his experiences Wordsworth did not commit to poetry until many years afterwards. 'Emotion recollected in tranquility' was how he himself described his way of composing.

THE ROAD TO BALA

We reached the top of the elevation.

'Yonder,' said my guide, pointing to a white bare place a great way off to the west, 'is Bala road.'

'Then I will not trouble you to go any further,' said I; 'I can find my way thither.'

'No, you could not,' said my guide; 'if you were to make straight for that place you would perhaps fall down a steep, or sink into a peat hole up to your middle, or lose your way and never find the road, for you would soon lose sight of that place, and from thence to Bala.' Thereupon he moved in a southerly direction down the steep and I followed him. In about twenty minutes we came to the road.

'Now,' said my guide, 'you are on the road; bear to the right and you cannot miss the way to Bala.'

'How far is it to Bala?' said I.

'About twelve miles.' he replied.

I gave him a trifle, asking at the same time if it was sufficient. 'Too much by one-half,' he replied; 'many, many thanks.' He then shook me by the hand, and accompanied by his dogs departed, not back over the moor, but in a southerly direction down the road.

Wending my course to the north, I came to the white bare spot which I had seen from the moor, and which was in fact the top of a considerable elevation over which the road passed. Here I turned and looked at the hills I had come across. There they stood, darkly blue, a rain cloud, like ink, hanging over their summits. Oh, the wild hills of Wales, the land of old renown and of wonder, the land of Arthur and Merlin!

The road now lay nearly due west. Rain came on, but it was at my back, so I expanded my umbrella, flung it over my shoulder and laughed. Oh, how a man laughs who has a good umbrella when he has the rain at his back, aye and over his head too, and at all times when it rains except when the rain is in his face, when the umbrella is not of much service. Oh, what a good friend to a man is an umbrella in rain time, and likewise at many other times. What need he fear if a wild bull or a ferocious dog attacks him, provided he has a good umbrella? He unfurls the umbrella in the face of the bull or dog, and the

'. . . I saw a valley below me with a narrow river running through it, to which
wooded hills sloped down; far to the west were blue mountains.'

The lake of Bala on a wild Welsh evening.

brute turns round quite scared, and runs away. Or if a footpad asks him for his money, what need he care provided he has an umbrella? He threatens to dodge the ferrule into the ruffian's eye, and the fellow stands back and says, 'Lord, sir! I meant no harm. I never saw you before in all my life. I merely meant a little fun.' Moreover, who doubts that you are a respectable character provided you have an umbrella? You go into a public-house and call for a pot of beer, and the publican puts it down before you with one hand without holding out the other for the money, for he sees that you have an umbrella and consequently property. And what respectable man, when you overtake him on the way and speak to him, will refuse to hold conversation with you, provided you have an umbrella? No one. The respectable man sees you have an umbrella, and concluded that you do not intend to rob him, and with justice, for robbers never carry an umbrella. Oh, a tent, a shield, a lance, and a voucher for character is an umbrella. Amongst the very best friends of man must be reckoned an umbrella.

The way lay over dreary, moory hills; at last it began to descend, and I saw a valley below me with a narrow river running through it, to which wooded hills sloped down; far to the west were blue mountains. The scene was beautiful but melancholy; the rain had passed away, but a gloomy almost November sky was above, and the mists of night were coming down apace.

I crossed a bridge at the bottom of the valley and presently saw a road branching to the right. I paused, but after a little time went straight forward. Gloomy woods were on each side of me and night had come down. Fear came upon me that I was not on the right road, but I saw no house at which I could inquire, nor did I see a single individual for miles of whom I could ask. At last I heard the sound of hatchets in a dingle on my right, and catching a glimpse of a gate at the head of a path, which led down into it, I got over it. After descending some time I hallooed. The noise of the hatchets ceased. I hallooed again, and a voice cried in Welsh, 'What do you want?' 'To know the way to Bala,' I replied. There was no answer, but presently I heard steps, and the figure of a man drew nigh, half undistinguishable in the darkness, and saluted me. I returned his salutation, and told him I wanted to know the way to Bala. He told me, and I found I had been going right. I thanked him and regained the road. I sped onward, and in about half-an-hour saw some houses, then a bridge, then a lake on my left, which I recognised as the lake of Bala. I skirted the end of it, and came to a street cheerfully lighted up, and in a minute more was in the White Lion Inn.

GEORGE BORROW,
Wild Wales.

RADNORSHIRE

Saturday, 26 February, 1870.
A lovely warm morning so I set off to walk over the hills to Colva, taking my luncheon in my pocket, half a dozen biscuits, two apples and a small flask of wine. Took also a pocket book and opera glasses. Went on up the Green Lane. Very hot walking. At the Green Lane Cottage found Mrs Jones and a daughter at home sewing. Price Price sitting half hidden in the chimney corner but alas there was no Abiasula

as the last time I was there. Price Price something like his sister Abiasula. A sturdy boy, with a round rosy good-humoured face and big black eyes, volunteered to guide me to Colva Church. So he came out of his chimney corner in the ingle nook and we started at once, accompanied by a grey and black sheepdog puppy. We were out on the open mountain at once. There was the brown withered heather, the elastic turf, the long green ride stretching over the hill like a green ribbon

Both man and beast find peace and tranquillity at this isolated Radnorshire church.

'. . . we crossed the Glasnant on a hurdle laid flat over the stream
and then we jumped the Arrow.'

between the dark heather. There was the free fresh fragrant air of the hills, but, oh, for the gipsy lassie with her wild dark eyes under her black hood. As we went down the Fualet a grouse cock uttered his squirling crow and flew over the crest of the hill. I never heard a grouse crow before. 'What's that bird crying?' I said to the boy. 'A grouse', he said, adding, 'There he goes over the bank. They be real thick hereabout'.

Tried to get across the swift Arrow (swollen by the junction of the Glasnant just above) by climbing along a rail but we failed and had to go up a meadow till we got above the meeting of the waters, when we crossed the Glasnant on a hurdle laid falt over the stream and then we jumped the Arrow. Up the steep breast of the Reallt to Dol Reallt and along the road to the Wern and Bryntwyn from whence a field path leads to Colva Church. Here Price Price left me after showing me across one field. I asked him to have some bread and cheese and beer at the Sun Inn, Colva, but he would not and could scarcely be prevailed on to take sixpence.

FRANCIS KILVERT,
Diary.

HURRAHING IN HARVEST

Summer ends now; now, barbarous in beauty, the stooks rise
Around; up above, what wind-walks! what lovely behaviour
Of silk-sack clouds! has wilder, wilful-wavier
Meal-drift moulded ever and melted across skies?

I walk, I lift up, I lift up heart, eyes,
Down all that glory in the heavens to glean our Saviour;
And, eyes, heart, what looks, what lips yet gave you a
Rapturous love's greeting of realer, of rounder replies?

And the azurous hung hills are his world-wielding shoulder
Majestic – as a stallion stalwart, very-violet-sweet! –
These things, these things were here and but the beholder
Wanting; which two when they once meet,
The heart rears wings bold and bolder
And hurls for him, O half hurls earth for him off under his feet.

GERARD MANLEY HOPKINS

Hopkins wrote in a letter to Robert Bridge that this sonnet was the outcome of half-an-hour of extreme enthusiasm as he walked home alone one day from fishing in the Elwy. The Elwy is in Denbighshire. For three years Hopkins was studying theology at St Beuno's near St Asaph. He also learned Welsh during this time.

DAYS THAT HAVE BEEN

Can I forget the sweet days that have been,
    When poetry first began to warm my blood;
When from the hills of Gwent I saw the earth
    Burned into two by Severn's silver flood:

When I would go alone at night to see
    The moonlight, like a big white butterfly,
Dreaming on that old castle near Caerleon,
    While at its side the Usk went softly by.

The beautiful countryside near St Asoph. St Beuno's college can be
seen peering through the trees on the right.

Hopkins wrote *Hurrahing in Harvest*, in which he perceives the glory
of God in nature, after an afternoon's fishing on the River Elwy.

When I would stare at lovely clouds in Heaven,
   Or watch them when reported by deep streams;
When feeling pressed like thunder, but would not
   Break into that grand music of my dreams?

Can I forget the sweet days that have been,
   The villages so green I have been in;
Llantarnam, Magor, Malpas, and Llanwern,
   Liswery, old Caerleon, and Alteryn?

Can I forget the banks of Malpas Brook,
   Or Ebbw's voice in such a wild delight,
As on he dashed with pebbles in his throat,
   Gurgling towards the sea with all his might?

Ah, when I see a leafy village now,
   I sigh and ask it for Llantarnam's green;
I ask each river where is Ebbw's voice –
   In memory of the sweet days that have been.

W H DAVIES

WALES

The night had almost come, and the rain had not ceased, among the hills of an unknown country. Behind me, twelve desolate miles of hill and sky away, was a village; and on the way to it, half-a-dozen farms; and before me were three or four houses scattered over two or three miles of winding lanes, with an inn and a church. The parson had just come away from his poultry, and as his wife crossed the road with her apron over her head, I asked where the inn was, and whether it had a room ready in the winter. Two minutes after she had seen me – if she could see in the dark lane – she had told me that if the inn had no room, I was not to go farther, but to stay at the vicarage. But the inn had a bed to spare, and there was good beer to be had by a great fire in a room shining with brass and pewter, and overhead guns and hams and hanks of wool; and the hostess was jocund, stout, and young, and not only talkative but anxious to be talked to, and she had that maternal kindness – or shall I call it the kindness of a very desirable aunt? – towards strangers, which I have always found in Welsh women, young and old, in the villages and on the moors. So there I stayed and listened to the rain and the fire and the landlady's rich, humming voice uttering and playing strange tricks with English. I was given a change of clothing as if I had asked and paid for it. Then I went to the vicarage, and because I said I loved Welsh hymns and Welsh voices the vicar and his wife and daughter, without unction or preparation or a piano, sang to me, taking parts, some tremendous hymns and some gay melodies, *Whence banished is the roughness of our years*, which made the rain outside seem April rain. They sang, and told me about the road I was to follow, until I had to go to my inn.

Next day, after paying what I liked at the inn, and promising the hostess that I would learn Welsh, I walked for twenty miles over stony roads gleaming with rain upon the white thorns and bloom on the sloes, and through woods where nothing brooded solemnly over grey moss and green moss on the untrodden, rotten wood, and up dry, ladder-like beds of brooks that served as paths, over peat and brindled grass, and along golden hazel hedges, where grew the last meadow-sweet with herb-robert and harebell and one wild rose, and above little valleys of lichened ash trees; and sometimes beneath me, and sometimes high above, the yellow birches waved in the rain like sunset clouds fettered to the ground and striving and caracoling in their fetters.

When I left on the next morning early, the farmer was

'When I would stare at lovely clouds in Heaven,
Or watch them when reported by deep streams . . .'

'. . . I walked for twenty miles over stony roads gleaming with rain . . .'

'. . . along golden hazel hedges, where grew the last meadow-sweet
with herb-robert and harebell and one wild rose . . .'

threshing with an oaken flail in his barn; but he stepped out to tell me what he knew of the way through the bogs and over the hills – for there was no road or path – and to beg me not to go, and to ask me to pay what I had paid at my former inn, for my lodging.

The next twenty miles were the simplest and most pleasant in the world. For nearly the whole way there was a farm in every two miles. I had to call at each to ask my way. At one, the farmer asked me in and sat me by his peat fire to get dry, and gave me good milk and butter and bread, and a sack for my shoulders, and a sense of perfect peace which was only disturbed when he found that I could not help him in the verses he was writing for a coming wedding. At another, the farmer wrote out a full list of the farms and landmarks on my way, lest I should forget, and gave me bread and butter and milk. At another, I had but to sit and get dry and watch an immeasurably ancient, still, and stately woman, her face bound with black silk which came under her chin like a stock, and moving only to give a smile of welcome and goodwill. At another, they added cheese to the usual meal, and made the peat one golden cone upon the hearth, and brewed a pale

drink which is called tea. Sometimes the shrill-voiced women, with no English, their hair flying in the wind, came out and shrieked and waved directions. In one of the houses I was privileged to go from the kitchen, with its dresser and innumerable jugs and four tea-services, to the drawing-room. It was a change that is probably more emphasized in Wales than elsewhere since the kitchens are pleasanter, the drawing-rooms more mysterious, than in England, I think. The room was cold, setting aside the temperature, and in spite of crimson in the upholstery and cowslip yellow in the wallpaper and dreary green on the floor. There was a stuffed heron; a large pathetic photograph of man and wife; framed verses; some antimacassars, and some Bibles ... The room was dedicated to the unknown God. The farmer did not understand it; he admired it completely, and with awe, reverencing it as priest his god, knowing that it never did him any good, and yet not knowing what evil might come if he were without it.

EDWARD THOMAS,
Beautiful Wales.

ORGANISING A WALK

Consider for a moment the qualities needed by one who has undertaken the organisation of a party of walkers – if a mixed party, so much the better. To perform his functions successfully he must be a combination of Cook's agent, weather-prophet, geographical specialist, Bradshaw expert, commissariat officer, guide, nurse, hostess, and chaperon. First he must arrange the day and time, and train, so as to suit everybody, which involves a hail of postcards, telephone conversations, and personal interviews. Then he must provide a fine day – by far his easiest task. Then he must arrange the route, his choice being limited only by the fact that each member of the party has his own views about pace, distance,

time for lunch, and character of country, agreeing only that there must be no undue hurrying or waiting for the train home at the end of the walk. Then his functions as guide begin: he must necessarily lead the party, while keeping an eye behind to see that no one is straggling; he must never show even a momentary hesitation as to the route; he must receive with gratitude and attention the suggestions of his companions, who don't care about the map, but are sure they came that way with their uncle some years ago, and are quite certain the guide is wrong; he must watch the time all through, making painful mental calculations of routes *and* distances; he must be sure, if the route passes any ancient churches, public-houses, or registry offices, that no members of the party whose tastes incline there to linger too long with irretrievable results; and unless and until the party have reached a proper taciturnity, he must originate and stimulate interesting conversation. If the walk continues into the late afternoon – as it will if the leader has an ounce of sporting instinct – he must find a suitable place for tea at exactly the right time, and finally march his party down to their train with not more than five minutes to wait.

ARTHUR SIDGWICK,
Walking Essays.

SCOTLAND

LINES WRITTEN IN THE HIGHLANDS AFTER A VISIT TO BURNS'S COUNTRY

There is a charm in footing slow across a silent plain,
Where patriot battle has been fought, where glory had the
    gain;
There is a pleasure on the heath where Druids old have been,
Where mantles grey have rustled by and swept the nettles
    green;
There is a joy in every spot made known by times of old,
New to the feet, although each tale a hundred times be told;
There is a deeper joy than all, more solemn in the heart,

More parching to the tongue than all, of more divine a smart,
When weary steps forget themselves upon a pleasant turf,
Upon hot sand, or flinty road, or sea-shore iron scurf,
Toward the castle or the cot, where long ago was born
One who was great through mortal days and died of fame
    unshorn!

JOHN KEATS

TOURING SCOTLAND

When I come into a large town, you know there is no putting one's knapsack into one's fob, so the people stare. We have been taken for spectacle-vendors, razor-sellers, jewellers, travelling linen-drapers, spies, excise men and many things I have no idea of. When I asked for leters at Port Patrick, the man asked 'What regiment?'

I have got wet through day after day; eaten oat-cake and drank whisky; walked up to my knees in bog; got a sore throat ... went up Ben Nevis and come down again; sometimes when I am rather tired, I lean rather languishly on a rock, and long for some famous beauty to get down from her palfrey, in passing, approach me with her saddle-bags and give me a dozen or two capital roast beef sandwiches.

JOHN KEATS
In a letter written from Inverness to Mrs Wylie the
mother of his sister-in-law.
6th August 1818.

A tranquil scene in the heart of what was Ayrshire – Burns's Country.

'There is a charm in footing slow across a silent plain,
Where patriot battle has been fought, where glory had the gain . . .'

The rocky and tortuous track up to the summit of Ben Nevis.

The last spring snows cling to Ben Nevis. Though not possessing a true peak, the tallest mountain in the land does have an awesome grandeur all its own.

WINTER

There is scarcely any earthly object gives me more – I don't
know if I should call it pleasure – than to walk in the sheltered
side of a wood on a cloudy winter day and hear a stormy wind
howling among the trees and raving o'er the plain. It exalts
me, enraptures me.

ROBERT BURNS

ON GOING A JOURNEY

One of the pleasantest things in the world is going a journey;
but I like to go by myself. I can enjoy society in a room; but out
of doors, nature is company enough for me. I am then never
less alone than when alone.

The fields his study, nature was his book.

I cannot see the wit of walking and talking at the same time.
When I am in the country, I wish to vegetate like the country. I
am not for criticising hedge-rows and black cattle. I go out of
town in order to forget the town and all that is in it. There are
those who for this purpose go to watering-places, and carry
the metropolis with them. I like elbow-room, and fewer
incumbrances. I like solitude, when I give myself up to it, for
the sake of solitude; nor do I ask for

a friend in my retreat,
Whom I may whisper solitude is sweet

The soul of a journey is liberty, perfect liberty, to think, feel,
do just as one pleases. We go a journey, chiefly to be free of all
impediments and of all inconveniences; to leave ourselves
behind, much more to get rid of others. It is because I want a
little breathing-space to muse on indifferent matters, where
Contemplation

May plume her feathers and let grow her wings,
That in the various bustle of resort
Were all too ruffled, and sometimes impair'd,

that I absent myself from the town for awhile, without feeling
at a loss the moment I am left by myself. Instead of a friend in a
post-chaise or in a Tilbury, to exchange good things with, and
vary the same stale topics over again, for once let me have a
truce with impertinence. Give me the clear blue sky over my
head, and the green turf beneath my feet, a winding road
before me, and a three hours' march to dinner – and then to
thinking! It is hard if I cannot start some game on these lone
heaths. I laugh, I run, I leap, I sing for joy. From the point of
yonder rolling cloud, I plunge into my past being, and revel
there, as the sun-burnt Indian plunges headlong into the wave
that wafts him to his native shore. Then long-forgotten things,
like 'sunken wrack and sunless treasuries,' burst upon my
eager sight, and I begin to feel, think, and be myself again.
Instead of an awkward silence, broken by attempts at wit or
dull common-places, mine is that undisturbed silence of the

For Burns the greatest pleasure was to walk '. . . in the sheltered side of
a wood on a cloudy winter day . . .'

heart which alone is perfect eloquence. No one likes puns, alliterations, antitheses, argument, and analysis better than I do; but I sometimes had rather be without them. 'Leave, oh, leave me to my repose;' I have just now other business in hand, which would seem idle to you, but is with me 'very stuff of the conscience.' Is not this wild rose sweet without a comment? Does not this daisy leap to my heart set in its coat of emerald? Yet if I were to explain to you the circumstance that has so endeared it to me, you would only smile. Had I not better then keep it to myself, and let it serve me to brood over, from here to yonder craggy point, and from thence onward to the far-distant horizon? I should be but bad company all that way, and therefore prefer being alone. I have heard it said that you may, when the moody fit comes on, walk or ride on by yourself, and indulge your reveries. But this looks like a breach of manners, a neglect of others and you are thinking all the time that you ought to rejoin your party.

In general, a good thing spoils out-of-door prospects: it should be reserved for Table-talk. Lamb is for this reason, I take it, the worst company in the world out-of-doors, because he is the best within. I grant, there is one subject on which it is pleasant to talk on a journey; and that is, what one shall have for supper when we get to our inn at night. The open air improves this sort of conversation or friendly altercation, by setting a keener edge on appetite. Every mile of the road heightens the flavour of the viands we expect at the end of it. How fine it is to enter some old town, walled and turreted just at the approach of night-fall, or to come to some straggling village, with the lights streaming through the surrounding gloom; and then after inquiring for the best entertainment that the place affords, to 'take one's ease at one's inn!' These eventful moments in our lives' history are too precious, too full of solid, heart-felt happiness to be frittered and dribbled away in imperfect sympathy. I would have them all to myself, and drain them to the last drop: they will do to talk of or to write about afterwards. What a delicate speculation it is, after drinking whole goblets of tea,

The cups that cheer, but not inebriate,

and letting the fumes ascend into the brain, to sit considering what we shall have for supper – eggs and a rasher, a rabbit smothered in onions, or an excellent veal-cutlet! Sancho in such a situation once fixed upon cow-heel; and his choice, though he could not help it, is not to be disparaged. Then, in the intervals of pictured scenery and Sandean contemplation, to catch the preparation and the stir in the kitchen – *Procul, O procul este profani!* These hours are sacred to silence and to musing, to be treasured up in the memory, and to feed the source of smiling thoughts hereafter. I would not waste them in idle talk; or if I must have the integrity of fancy broken in upon, I would rather it were by a stranger than a friend. A stranger takes his hue and character from the time and place; he is a part of the furniture and costume of an inn. If he is a Quaker, or from the West Riding of Yorkshire, so much the better. I do not even try to sympathise with him, and he breaks no squares. I associate nothing with my travelling companion but present objects and passing events. In his ignorance of me and my affairs, I in a manner forget myself. But a friend reminds one of other things, rips up old grievances, and destroys the abstraction of the scene. He comes in ungraciously between us and our imaginary character.

WILLIAM HAZLITT,
Table Talk.

ACKNOWLEDGEMENTS

The publishers wish to thank the following for permission to quote extracts.

The Estate of W H Davies *The Complete Poems of W H Davies* published by Jonathan Cape Ltd, United Kingdom, and Wesleyan University Press, U S A.

The Estate of Eleanor Farjeon: *Edward Thomas: The Last Four Years* published by Oxford University Press.

G M Trevelyan: *Walking* and *The Middle Marches* published by Methuen & Co.

Every effort has been made to contact the owners of the copyright of all the information contained in this book, but if, for any reason, any acknowledgements have been omitted, the publishers ask those concerned to contact them.